D1440930

CURBSIDE SPLENDOR PUBLISHING

Published by Curbside Splendor Publishing, Inc., Chicago, Illinois
in 2014.

First Edition
Copyright © 2014 by Tim Kinsella

Library of Congress Control Number: 2014933481

ISBN 978-1-940430-01-0

Edited by Mairead Case
Design by Zach Dodson at Bleached Whale Design
Cover Illustration by Beth Hoeckel
Interior Illustration by Melina Ausikaitis

Set in Georgia

Manufactured in the United States of America.

www.curbsidesplendor.com

Let Go and Go On and On

A Novel

Based on the roles of Laurie Bird

Tim Kinsella

For Mary Jennifer Buffett

foreword

It is well known that at the 1973 Academy Awards, Marlon Brando, protesting Hollywood's depiction of Native Americans, sent an actress dressed as an Apache to decline his Best Actor Award.

It is less well remembered, however, that later in the night, Clint Eastwood jokingly refused to present the Best Picture Award "on behalf of all the cowboys who have gotten shot in John Ford Westerns."

This was after *Easy Rider* and before *Star Wars*, but still the Nixon years.

Brando's truant activism had a twinge of poetic obscurity.

But with his cavalier remark, Dirty Harry reinstated the norm: the movies just entertainment, free from ideology.

*

Before its release, the screenplay of *Two-Lane Blacktop* was published in full in *Esquire,* with the headline "The Movie of the Year."

Rolling Stone published a story about the making of the film.

And when completed, it was reputed to be the head of Universal's least favorite movie ever made.

Until becoming available as a Criterion Collection DVD in 2007, the film survived obscurely on VHS, often bootlegged and traded, handed over as if granting initiation into a select cult.

After the commercial failure of *Two-Lane Blacktop*, its director Monte Hellman next found work back in the B-movie market where he had come up.

Cockfighter was a Roger Corman production, cranked out quick and cheap for drive-ins.

Just as he had in *Two-Lane Blacktop*, in *Cockfighter* Hellman dealt with quiet, obsession, subculture, and definitions of masculinity.

As of this writing, *Cockfighter* is available on DVD only as a double feature with an exploitation film about an erotic women's prison.

*

Annie Hall won the Academy Award for Best Picture.

It also introduced the phrase "visible panty line" into the American lexicon, and also the concept of considering a relationship as a shark.

Bad Timing, directed by Nicolas Roeg, won The London Film Critic Circle's Award for Best Director.

One of the executives at its UK distributor called it "a sick film made by sick people for sick people."

The distributor's logo was removed from all UK prints of the film.

With *Performance*, *Walkabout*, and *Don't Look Now*, Roeg had already proven himself to be an innovative director with a bias for fractured mosaic structures.

And though his approaches differed significantly from Hellman's, Roeg also crafted layered and complex films that sought to investigate alienation, obsession, subculture, and definitions of masculinity.

*

Laurie Bird, a principal actress in *Two-Lane Blacktop* and *Cockfighter,* had a small role in *Annie Hall,* playing Paul Simon's girlfriend.

Later, she was engaged to marry Art Garfunkel.

She committed suicide in their New York penthouse at the age of twenty-five, while he was on location in Vienna shooting *Bad Timing*, a film which ironically mimics her own tragedy.

Very little is known about her.

Very little remains besides her films.

There are some clues in Garfunkel's book of poems *Stillwater*, which is dedicated to her.

There are some screen tests for *Two-Lane Blacktop,* and a couple of her stoned journal entries.

But mostly there are holes and mysteries.

Through a thread of films spanning the 1970s, Bird represents the domestication of a Dionysian ideal: a beautiful androgynous hitchhiker settling down into the role of a politely gendered wife, and rewarded with upward social mobility for doing so.

But ultimately, one archetypical role defined her legacy: the tragic starlet.

*

This book by no means intends to convey any *truth* beyond one possible solution to the puzzles of her life and work.

It gleefully plays dumb to the simple facts of life on earth, proper sampling etiquettes, and the philosophical constraints of both freewill and predetermination.

I humbly appropriate the works of Hellman and Roeg as elements of my own.

Their daringness and trust in their audience inspired me as a young man, and guided my work here.

*

prologue: BLOWUP

Michaelangelo Antonioni made his first English language film, *Blowup,* in 1966.

In it, David Hemmings is a fashion photographer eager to make some greater artistic statement.

He refers to all women as either "birds" or "bitches."

The film begins with a Jeep, overstuffed with mimes in checkered patterns and top hats, all flailing wildly as the car zigzags.

But they aren't exactly mimes because, crammed in there like it's an open-topped clown car, they all scream and holler.

They park and run the streets giddy, attacking the traffic with laughter.

And unshaven, in torn pants and a torn coat, David leaves a factory alongside other silent workers, all crammed together to pass through a wet metal and stone gate.

Once he knows that no one is watching, David jumps into his convertible and gets his secretary on the C.B.

He sticks his camera in the glove compartment.

The smiling mimes attack him in his convertible, and he returns to a house busy with activity.

*

Models hang out in their underwear together, and change tops with the door open.

One model dressed in sequins is waiting for David.

A bottle of wine is already opened.

David approaches, teasing her with big feathers.

Her sides exposed fully, her ribs are like fingers.

Her shoulders and hipbones are pronounced and knobby.

David's assistant loads the cameras and hands them back off.

The pace accelerates as David shoots, and he gets closer and closer to the model until eventually, they're only a foot apart and he's ranting.

– *Good. Good. Great. Hold that. Again. Good. Work. Work. Work. Great. Arms up.*

He mounts her and kisses her while continuing to shoot.

He says – *Head Up.*

His shirt is unbuttoned and she's on her back on the floor. Finishing, he relaxes as if he'd just climaxed.

He makes his assistant talk on the phone for him while he lies back on the couch and looks off into space.

*

David gets ready like he's going on a date.

While he shaves, another assistant brings him a contact sheet to look at.

Throwing away the rags that he'd worn to the factory, he puts on white pants and a baby blue shirt, tucked in and unbuttoned low.

He's gruff with the models in peacock costumes and jockey outfits. – *No chewing gum.*

Pulling at their legs rough, he says – *Mouth open, eyes over here.*

He shouts in their faces to get a startled reaction.

He bosses his whole world around according to how it fits within his frame.

Bored, he tells all the models and his assistants to close their eyes.

Then he walks off and leaves them waiting while he visits his friend next door, an abstract expressionist painter.

*

The Abstract Expressionist tells him – *I don't mean anything when I do them. Afterwards I find something to hang on to.*

The Abstract Expressionist says – *It sorts itself out. It*

adds up.

Sarah Miles brings David a beer and massages his head.

Maybe she is his wife.

The way the film is shot, everything is seen through stripes and behind layers, wood blinds.

The frame continuously changes shapes.

*

As David leaves the studio, Jane Birkin and her friend ask to speak with him.

They are aspiring models.

With his feet up on his desk, he rolls a quarter between his fingers while they talk.

He's got sleepy eyes like Michael Caine.

*

He drives fast through streets in which first every building is painted red, and then every building is painted blue.

He stops in a neighborhood in which every building is stone.

In the antique shop full of headless statues and plaster busts and pieces of marble, the old man working there tells him – *There are no cheap bargains here* – and blows dust into David's face.

So David grabs his camera and wanders into the park.

Little is happening, and the park is silent except for the birds and the patterned soft whack of a tennis game.

David chases the birds when they land, and shoots them as they take off away from him.

*

Vanessa Redgrave and an older man saunter up a slope into the bushes, and David hops and clicks his heels as he follows them.

The couple is playful and affectionate in a clearing.

Stepping over a fence to hide in the bushes, David shoots the couple.

He moves closer and stands behind a tree, and then he's not very far at all and he's shooting them.

They're distracted by their kisses.

Vanessa looks around, but the man looks only at her.

For a long time it is silent, except for the breeze through the trees and the small clicking of the camera.

Finally, Vanessa notices David and chases after him, away from the clearing and down some steps.

She is furious and insists that he stop photographing them.

She says – *This is a public place. Everyone has a right to be left in peace.*

It's not my fault if there's no peace. – He replies.

She falls to the ground and bites his hand to grab the camera from him.

She says – *You've never seen me.* – And runs away.

*

Back at the antique store, David talks to the young girl who works there.

It seems maybe he's scouting her to be a model.

She says that she's fed up with antiques and wants to head off to Nepal or Morocco.

But their conversation is cut short when he falls irrepressibly in love with a big wooden propeller buried in the stacks that he insists he needs at that very moment.

He tries to throw it in the back of his convertible, but the girl says she'll get it delivered to him later that day.

It turns out that he wants to buy the junk shop.

He tells his secretary that he thinks the property value will go up because he sees queers with poodles walking around.

*

David delivers his photos of the factory workers to his agent, a man in a suit eating a very fancy lunch alone in a restaurant.

The factory workers are naked in some of the photos, and changing into their work clothes in others.

To order his lunch, David touches the waiter's arm as he walks past.

He tells his agent – *I wish I had a ton of money. Then I'd be free.*

Through the window, he notices a strange man looking around in his convertible.

Before his lunch even arrives, he runs from the restaurant to follow the man.

He lays on the horn constantly when driving.

But a parade of protestors carrying hand made signs against nuclear weapons walks by in silence and he waves them past, waits for them to cross.

*

When he arrives back at his studio, Vanessa shows up to get the film from him.

He puts on some Herbie Hancock music and offers her a drink as if it's a sudden afternoon seduction.

They argue about who has the ultimate rights: the photographer, or the subject of a photo.

He tells her that she should be a model and stands her up against a purple background.

He takes his coat off and commands her to sit next to him.

His wife, presumably Sarah Miles, calls and he tries to make Vanessa talk to her.

He sets a smoldering match down on the head of a statue and pets it affectionately.

He explains to Vanessa that beautiful women are boring objects.

She says it's the same with men.

But he cuts her off to insist that she listens to this Herbie Hancock song, and that she remain still when doing so.

He commands her to smoke slowly and against the beat.

She asks him for a glass of water and when he steps away to get it, she tries to run off with his camera, but he is waiting for her at the door.

She takes off her shirt and offers him sex in exchange for the film.

He tells her that he's not interested.

He offers her the negatives, but secretly switches the roll of film that he hands her.

Once he hands her the film, then they kiss and head off to bed.

But someone rings the bell, and David answers the door topless.

His propeller is delivered.

They get high topless together in the afternoon and think of the propeller as a sculpture.

Saying goodbye, he asks her name.

She won't say it, but writes down a false phone number.

At this point, there is a big piece of lint right in the lower center of the frame.

It is navy blue and curly.

*

When she leaves, he immediately develops the film to see why she was so anxious about retrieving it.

For the process of printing out big photos, he uses a magnifying glass and big metal contraptions.

Blown up, the photos are grainy, but the look of concern on Vanessa's face is apparent.

David has to blow up a small detail over and over.

Maybe he realizes that he never saw the man again, after Vanessa chased him away.

It takes a long time and many steps of blowing the image up more and more.

A central question of the film might be why David, who obviously has a very busy schedule, would get so lost in pursuing this.

Finally, grainy and obscure, he sees it.

A man is behind the fence.

He reconsiders the whole sequence of events slowly before

making out exactly what he's looking at: a gun in the man's hand.

He calls his agent first, certain and excited that just his mere presence with a camera that day has saved a life.

But before he can explain this to his agent, he is disturbed again by someone else at the door.

*

It is the aspiring teenage models again, Jane Birkin and her friend.

He commands them to make him a coffee, and they sneak off to try on some clothes.

When he catches them topless, he pulls Jane Birkin's hair and starts biting her until they are all three on top of the knocked over clothes racks and tearing the clothes all apart.

Then they tear apart the big purple backdrop.

The girls are both naked in the rumble of the giant purple paper, choking him with their green stockings, giggling and screaming.

*

The girls dress him.

And waking up, shirt open and fresh from a three-way, David becomes distracted again by the blown up photos.

Shooing the girls, he finally realizes that he has witnessed a murder.

*

It is night, and he drives back to the park alone to find the corpse.

In the wet green grass, the body is a shadow under a tree; eyes wide open in the moonlight.

But David has forgotten his camera.

He is scared off by a twig snapping.

*

Returning home, David finds Sarah Miles under his friend The Abstract Expressionist, making love.

He and she make eye contact, but he walks out without saying anything.

Returning to his studio he finds that all the negatives and enlargements that show the murder have been stolen.

His dark room is destroyed.

One grainy print of the corpse was left behind, forgotten beside the sink.

When Sarah Miles comes to find him in his studio, he calmly tells her that he saw a man get murdered this morning.

Who was he?

Someone.

He shows her the print and says – *That's the body.*

She says it looks like one of The Abstract Expressionist's paintings.

*

David heads off to pick up his agent, to show him the body, and he sees Vanessa in the street.

He pulls over to chase her and ends up down dark alleys, and in a rock club where one hundred completely stoic and expressionless kids are watching The Yardbirds with Jeff Beck and Jimmy Page.

Except for one biracial couple dancing, everyone is entirely catatonic.

Jeff Beck has trouble with his amp, his cable shorting when he tries to solo.

Frustrated, he bangs his guitar against his amp and destroys it and once he stomps on his guitar and throws it into the crowd, the audience gets excited and there's a near-riot.

The band continues to play through all of this.

David catches the neck of the guitar and gets chased for it.

Dropping it on the street, a kid picks it up, interested for a second, but not knowing that it's Jeff Beck's, the kid drops it.

*

David shows up at a party to track down his agent.

It's smoky and there's lots of fringe, people in suits sitting on pillows.

Beautiful young people with money are beautiful stoned.

His agent is in a dark corner with some young girls.

David turns down a puff of a joint.

He wants the agent to go with him to take a photo of the corpse.

But the agent is too stoned to understand anything that David tells him.

*

David wakes up in the party aftermath.

It is silent, very early, bottles and garbage everywhere.

He returns to the park to photograph the corpse.

But the corpse is gone.

The grass is not even flattened.

The park is quiet enough that the wind through the trees is rustling.

Everything is green.

And also up early is the Jeep crammed full of screaming mimes, speeding through the park wildly, waving handkerchiefs and flailing.

No one else is in the park to see it except David.

The Jeep parks, and two of the mimes overtake the tennis court.

The other mimes are all thrilled to press up against the fence and watch the mimed game of tennis.

Turning their heads to follow the imaginary ball, they ignore David.

With their eyes, they all follow the volley back and forth over the net.

The players are lobbing it high and swinging big overhand.

And then the imaginary ball goes over the fence.

All the mimes look to David to return the imaginary ball.

He trots off across the field and complies, hopping a few steps to get it high over the tall fence.

His eyes follow the ball and the sound of the ball being played is heard.

*

A few years after its release, you saw this film when you were living in Manhattan.

*

LET GO AND GO ON AND ON

PART 1

Two-Lane Blacktop

(1971)

You woke up startled in the high-contrast autumn dawn, to the patter of rain on the car's sheet metal roof.

It was loud, and sounded like dry rice being poured into a cheap pan.

Below you, the continuous rolling growl of the engine.

All of the innumerable variations of sleep do have one thing in common: you only know you're sleeping when you wake up a little.

Even lucid dreaming, that's true.

And lucid dreaming might not be a bad way to understand how you made your way through the world.

You were neither sleepwalking nor merely lucid.

And especially then, at seventeen, you were sensual perfection at its most muted.

Bent up in the backseat, your faded jeans had twisted at the waist.

Your knees ached.

You needed to keep stretching just to keep still.

You pulled your scratchy green army coat up close against your freezing cheeks, and you couldn't tell, but maybe the smell of motor oil had saturated your jacket more than it had the rest of the car.

*

James did all the driving.

Tall and bony; and his black hair hung chin-length, a little longer in the back.

Dennis sat shotgun, maybe awake.

Stocky and dusty blond, Dennis had the chin of a five-star-general and wide sideburns cutting down close to the edges of his face.

Both men were silent.

You didn't know their names yet.

Waking weird, the time warp of sleeping in motion, you thought it could've been Oklahoma already, maybe even Arkansas.

You were in a place where the roads go straight ahead.

Tall antennas scratched up into the low sky like robot trees among the other various species of trees planted alongside one another.

Cattle stood dumb among the sparse white flowers in the black field.

The metal machinery in the mud was painted beige to camouflage it in a desert landscape.

You figured this was probably only Texas.

*

You'd driven all night after driving since the morning before, about twenty-two hours since taking off from Santa Fe.

The sustained silence had a cumulative effect: that total loss of short-term memory that comes hard from looking out a silent window.

Every singular moment of the continuous hours had its own immersive display: The meander and warble of the beams in unison with the curves of the dark road; a long series of barns all built in a similar style each collapsed differently.

Every time you passed a harshly-lit low billboard, the blankness of your own expression, reflected faintly on the window over quivering flashes of the moon, stunned you.

Your mind, so flipping and agile, was somehow hidden behind such a dull gaze.

Like any one bubble within a foam, each instant of those silent hours expanded until it burst.

And finally, the dissipating hours lifted like a mist.

*

Waiting for each of your senses to knock back into position, it took you a long while to adjust to being conscious again.

Everything ached.

Everything fuzzy and throbbing, the silent hours had buried your voice, internalized you.

You understood their silence – the men's – the momentum of their daze.

When you met them only two days before, or one day maybe, as travel days smeared into one another, their shared daze spooked you a little.

But in a way you found it charming.

You sat up, goose bumps up your arms and throat clenched.

Cracking that silence, you told them simply, you said – *It's cold in here.*

But its shell – The Silence – had hardened layer upon layer each minute that had passed.

The men had both retreated too far down inside themselves to return quickly to the surface.

You understood they weren't exactly ignoring you.

You let your remark dangle.

They both remained blank.

It's freezing in here, what gives? – You said.

Dennis sighed.

Being friendly, at least cordial, seemed to come more easily to Dennis.

Maybe he had shallower depths to return from.

James was able to blink, but that was it.

Dennis glanced over his shoulder at you, but turned back toward the road ahead before speaking. – *No heat. Slows it down.*

Jesus Christ. – You said. – *You guys are something. You know that?*

Using your fuzzy purse as a pillow, you laid back down, pulled your jacket back up around your ears.

The rain shook on the glass, clinging together in tiny splotches.

You closed your eyes, your sense of time passing obliterated, you didn't know for how long.

And, though hypnotized by the whiz of the road passing under you, you didn't – couldn't – fall back asleep.

*

You sat up and massaged Dennis's shoulders.

Gripping hard, you felt his flannel shirt slip and bunch against muscle.

But even after so many hours silent and still, he didn't acknowledge your touch with so much as a flinch.

Looking at James in profile, you kept at it, massaging Dennis's shoulders.

You kept at it like you didn't notice Dennis not noticing you.

I'm hungry. – You said, easing up on your grip and petting his shoulders to smooth down his shirt.

We're stopping soon – he replied. – *Gotta pick up that piston.*

How soon? – You asked, your palms flat on his shoulders.

I don't know. – He said. – *Two, three hours.*

Suppressing a sigh, improvising a fake yawn, you laid back down and flipped around backwards on the small seat, attempting some variation in your bend.

All you wanted was to settle your hip somewhere in-between, away from all the lumps and bolts scattered under the thin, torn foam.

*

You had been on your way to the Grand Canyon with some guy, or you were supposed to have been.

He said you'd get there.

But he kept pulling over to the side of the road and getting stoned so much that you two weren't going anywhere.

You didn't know him enough to know if this was how he always was.

His hearse-looking truck painted psychedelic – a flat, contained design on a black-steel field – was impossible to get comfortable in.

30

Sitting around roadside in the beating sun, he'd paw at you.

Crowd you.

Even with all his talk of openness and freedom, he'd crowd you.

And since leaving New York, you'd been so relieved to not think about how you looked.

The same big gray T-shirt didn't need much washing.

Your red hair was thick, and playing with it enough to prevent it from getting matted was all the styling you felt necessary.

But, smoking so much weed in such tight quarters with this guy, the paranoia kept creeping up on you.

In some diner's parking lot, he slept sitting up in the driver's seat.

With a dusty thud, you threw your heavy bag to the gravel.

He kept the passenger-side door shut by tying it closed with a rope.

You dealt with that and climbed out.

You picked up your bag, and threw it through the open window of this denim-blue, souped-up '55 Chevy parked next to you.

*

Not just *Not-Flashy*, The 55 had been stripped of all decorative markings, transformed into austere minimalism.

Without ornamentation of any sort, its matte finish and its shape, all slow curves, were strange as a shark.

The only conspicuous modification: a big odometer, you guessed, bolted to the dash, which appeared filched from a submarine's control room.

You stowed-away quiet in the backseat, small and alert, waiting to see who'd step out of the diner and get in.

It had to be someone cool.

If they weren't cool they wouldn't have a car like that.

Two guys a little older than you, Dennis and James, approached, motor oil smeared into their torn clothes.

Dennis got in first, shotgun.

He looked at you but turned away quick and remained silent, without even a shrug or blink of acknowledgement.

Dennis glanced to James as James climbed in, but James didn't even look at you before pulling off, still silent – no hello, not even a look of surprise.

None.

Dust blew up into thick, lingering clouds behind the car.

*

Finally, resituating your weight after sitting some minutes, you had to say – *Hey it's really bumpy back here.*

Neither of the men responded or even glanced back at you. They were silent, eyes on the road.

What kind of car is this anyway? – You asked.

Silent, eyes on the road.

Up against their silence, that paranoia that you'd hoped to ditch back with that psychedelic truck came swelling up again.

Maybe they really hadn't seen you.

Maybe you'd been smoking so much, maybe you really had become invisible.

You'd know if you didn't exist.

Wouldn't you?

Assuming you did still exist, if you hadn't faded and they could still see you, what kind of guys wouldn't even acknowledge you with a nod?

– *You guys aren't the Zodiac Killers, are you?*

Dennis half-spun around in his seat and smiled.

His eyes kind, he held his gaze on you a moment.

He said – *Just passing through* – as if that answered your question.

And he turned back to the road ahead, the road as if projected up on a screen.

Staring straight ahead, the three of you sat silent in the car's immersive roar.

Which way we going? – You asked, simplifying your line of questioning.

The men had to at least acknowledge that you were moving. *East.* – Dennis said, without turning around.

And though you'd grown up in Long Island and this drift of yours began when you left New York City only the year before, you responded – *Cool.*

You didn't know why you said it, why you lied, but you said – *Cool, I've never been East before.*

*

Pulling into Santa Fe, the men had three hundred racing bread, and twenty to spare.

You had nothing.

Dennis not only did all the work, even most of the heavy lifting alone, but he also navigated whenever the car pulled into a town.

None of his directions gave you any reason to believe that he had any more knowledge of Santa Fe than James did.

Apparently he navigated by no greater authority than his own hunches.

But still, James submitted to his authority.

*

In the touristy, old city center, among generations of Mexican women with their hand-spun carpets and beads, you felt yourself the center from which various overlapping mud brick patterns uncoiled.

You passed the afternoon's dwindling hours asking the arty old squares and families, milling about, for spare change.

Though you'd picked up the habit out of necessity, you enjoyed it: approaching strangers, meeting people and disarming them with immediate kindness, humility.

You told people that you needed a bus back to San Francisco. – *I got sick and had to use the allowance my parents gave me.*

*

Shortly after dark you met back up with the guys to cruise the drive-in.

Rolling slowly through the lot, Dennis mumbled narration.

– *A '70 Camaro*

– *... A '68 Barracuda*

– *... Some muscle here*

– *A '32 Ford with a Four-Twenty-Seven ...*

– *... Eleven-inch rubber in the rear.*

Even at a crawl, the growl of The 55 must've been intimidating.

People watched you pass, hushed.

His voice no louder than his breath – *All we got to do is roll one.* – Dennis said.

Moving right up into the middle of things, James parked and you all got out.

A few people gathered around The 55.

– *Chevy block Four-Fifty-Four, four-speed trans, double-headers.*

*

Demonstratively not-in-a-hurry, sly, you three meandered.

With challenges and taunts in codes, his voice a modest drawl, James knew how to provoke a race.

The most you had ever heard him speak:

– *Not bad for homegrown.*

– *Gee Mister, must be pretty quick.*

You fell in easily with those two.

It wasn't alarming to imagine having to sleep with either of them.

Maybe they reminded you of your brother, but not too much.

Even as much as you enjoyed watching them, set apart like an audience by the conclusive fact that you had no idea what they were talking about, you still felt a part of their gang.

And you liked the idea of anticipating how fast something was only by looking at it at rest.

All at once, you understood in your gut why fast cars are sexy.

The same gaze translates.

The same gaze considers a body at rest, its parts as parts, and how these parts all come together with unified intent, imagining the body's performance.

All suspense.

All potential.

*

James worked a local with a catfish-looking mustache up into a rage.

And so they would race.

The entire lot formed a parade out to Airport Road, the last mile a dramatic crawl.

Its streetlights dim, the dark road was lit by headlights alone.

Parked, people scurried and stumbled around The 55, headless unless they bent down into the beams.

Without faces, only their subtle uniforms were visible.

Everyone wore one of the same couple cuts of jeans, but matching patches clarified allegiances.

A crowd gathered around for The 55's transformation.

Obviously part of the performance, moving symmetrically, James helped Dennis disassemble the car's extra weight with a silent, complex choreography.

The hood unhinged behind the front wheel, low next to the door.

The trunk, a flimsy metal sheet, lifted off.

Some trusted third-party inspected the cars and held the money.

The cars in position, the yellow stripe of the road stretched ahead in their beams.

You liked the smell of the oil and peeling rubber.

The roar of the engines drowned out all sound that the excited crowd might've made, made everyone pull close to shout into each other's ears.

The smoke, low on the pavement, made the crowd appear as if in a dream and faraway.

Through this cloud, the organizers blinked their flashlight-semaphore language.

And as the cars passed them, the people all fanned out across the road in a unified motion like a wave or a flag clapping in the wind.

*

You liked Dennis and James.

Compared to the put-on of the street-racer greaser-slicks they faced, the depoliticized Panther-cool of all those hot-rod types, not only James in his wool turtleneck, but even Dennis in his denim jacket appeared humble, if not frumpy.

The racing consumed them, the driving and the racing.

Most of those other people seemed to just be into the fashion of racing.

You could tell the difference.

*

Pulling back into the old downtown late, the guys agreed to splurge with the prize money and get a motel room.

You rarely even thought about wanting money anymore, and had become accustomed to plenty of discomforts.

You didn't want to owe anyone anything.

But you were happy to share their room.

James jumped out of the car at a red light.

He stared weird at you, lingering at the open door in the middle of the street as the light turned green.

Dennis slid across the bench to the driver's seat.

You stayed in back.

James said he'd check out a couple bars.

Wound up, he felt like sitting alone in a crowd.

Said he'd walk over to the motel later.

Stepping past mannequins in the Woolworth's lit-up windows, his silhouette was strange, lanky past decapitated heads in the hat store's display.

*

You'd been considering which of the guys you'd prefer to make it with.

But as long as you were all three hanging out together, you thought that maybe it wouldn't happen.

Symbiotic as the guys may have been, they never gave you the impression that they were kinky with each other.

That night you didn't particularly feel like balling.

You were tired.

And of course you hadn't recognized the unspoken code between them, but you were a little bit relieved that the guys had negotiated which one of them would split and leave the other one alone with you.

Choosing would've been the most exhausting part.

You probably wanted James to compete for you, angle himself strategically against Dennis.

But you understood that not competing had more to do with the guys' relationship with each other than it did with either one of them and you.

Maybe you would've liked to be desired enough to make James risk something.

But that was probably only your conceptual desire.

In actuality, you hardly felt much preference either way.

So maybe it was just that the men had decided you were Dennis's for the night without even consulting you, but once you were alone with Dennis you felt you probably would've preferred James.

The thought of you with anyone else ...

*

You two were clumsy getting started.

That's not uncommon.

Silent, Dennis laid spread out on his back on the bed, his eyes on the cracked plaster ceiling, never even turning to look at you.

After all that noise, the entire day and night before and all that morning with the rumble of the engine and the whir of the road, with downtown's crush of tourists and the radios

37

among the crowds at the race, the silence of the motel room hit you hard.

It felt oppressive, like every little move you made was too loud and clumsy.

Dennis was sticky with sweat and oil.

And you didn't know what the hell was on his mind, what with that stupid, bemused smirk all the time.

His stupid default expression: vacant smirking.

It got weirder the more it remained.

James did all the driving, travel and racing, so you guessed that maybe Dennis got some kind of satisfaction just being the mechanic, which, maybe you thought was maybe kind of mysterious or interesting.

Sprawled out in his dirty clothes over the comforter, he never even looked at you.

You unpacked, did some light organizing.

The tap of drawers closing and the whoosh of the curtain's rings against its rail were clunky loud.

You flinched when your arm brushed against the greasy patterned curtain.

Dennis looked dirty, like anywhere that his body folded he would stick to himself.

He moved to one side of the bed, lay with his hands behind his head as you undid the bedding at the other top corner.

It was a tricky bed to get into, layers of sheets and blankets to unfold just right.

He'd un-tucked his T-shirt from his jeans before laying down, but tucked it back in when he hopped up to help you fold back the bedding.

You both remained silent.

You wondered if you would hear James at the door when he arrived.

*

Driving, until you stopped in Santa Fe, you'd flipped back and forth being comfortable or not with their silence.

It'd creep you out.

You'd sing to yourself in the backseat.

Then you'd appreciate the silence for a while, how tiny the codes between the guys could shrink down to.

That intimacy of habit, that was interesting to watch.

But at the motel, Dennis might have been cute, but if you were about to screw him, that silence made you uneasy.

Not suspenseful and in no way a turn-on, it only made you uneasy.

A good romp, you felt, especially the first time with someone, it was all about communication.

Standing there, the blankets folded back, the silence thickening between you two, panicking, you considered voices: a persona to slip into, some litany of swears, filth to loosen him up.

But that wasn't your style.

Communication didn't mean playacting.

And you'd never had any hangups.

That was the thing about you that people liked.

You didn't hold back or flinch or compromise, and you put up no false fronts.

And you made your openness appear effortless.

But without the bluster of the engine and the woof of the wind, Dennis's silence felt amplified.

Overlapping waves of crickets chirped outside.

Finally, pressed together chest-to-chest, next to the bed, you kissed him.

There was an audible smacking of lips.

The least gasp or sigh you might let slip would crack through the whole motel like a wail.

You licked at his lips, your fingers through the back of his hair.

No louder than a breath, you moaned.

You hoped that maybe after a strained minute, your sounds might become involuntary.

Your voice in your chest might climb up into your throat, you hoped, and rupture with a squeak.

And with his calloused hands slow and steady on your lower back, the back of your neck, he smirked that stupid smirk.

*

On your back crossing the desert, sprawled out in the lumpy backseat, peaks of sandy jagged stone rolled past, cutting against flat blue sky, framed by the window and the ceiling.

In New Mexico the telephone poles go off and just keep going.

A poster of an afro'd toddler-angel taped to the backseat crinkled against your side.

However weird and quiet the guys had been the day before, driving all day, you expected that by that morning, and leaving Santa Fe, they would've gotten over it.

You didn't realize that the silence was a shared state between them that they returned to each morning, hitting reset.

*

You said – *Why can't I ever sit up front? What is this anyways, some kind of masculine power trip? I'm shoved back here with these goddamn tools.*

You'd been swapping rides constantly and even when a stranger sometimes welcomed you with a hint of menace, that was still at least showing you the respect of some special attention.

Even the playful mocking of your voice, which happened all the time with new people – it always shocked people how low your voice was – at least that was something, an acknowledgement of some kind.

These guys just remained silent.

You seemed to be tracking the surface of some well-lit moon.

You were bored.

You said – *Screwdrivers and wrenches don't make it for me, you know?*

Ignoring you, Dennis turned to James, said – *She's not breathing right, might be the jets.*

40

James nodded.

Dennis continued. – *We'll need bread to do a little work on the carburetors and check out the rear end.*

I don't see anybody paying attention to my rear end. – You said.

You thought you were being pretty funny.

But still they ignored you.

Neither of them even smirked, zero acknowledgement that they'd even heard you.

You told them that you had to take a leak.

They'd have to consent to that.

Such a request required specific action.

They opened the car up for a short sprint, Dennis listening close to the engine and James wanting to get a sense of its feel.

After all, it was a car made and optimized for sprints, not marathons.

Something must've been iffy, the stress of the race the night before, maybe something with the engine.

You didn't know what Dennis heard or what James felt, but they pushed it to full throttle, then let the car rest a few times before pulling over.

*

Pulled over on the side of the road, Dennis fooled around with something, a "foul plug" under the hood.

You and James sat in the dirt between brushy little splotches of dead grass.

Across the road and up ahead a little ways, a fossil of a blown-out tire curled like a thick rubber ribbon.

It was the first time that you and James had ever sat alone even for a minute.

The flat heat and vast silence between you two was strange after a couple days around each other all the time.

Like the shock of the motel room the night before, the desert's silence was made deeper by following the holler and bump of the wind and the engine.

You wanted to ask who owned the car, but didn't.

He stared at you.

In the distance, a thick blue stripe of rain appeared darker than the blue around it, angling between the ground and a cloud only halfway up into the sky.

*

Dennis the vacant stud executed his perfected touch with such grace.

Practiced but intuitive, he always knew the exact right pressure to apply.

Confident that he would never not find work, his simple skills added weight to his unconscious step and unthinking extra inches whenever he'd spread himself out in any shared space like a man far taller than he actually stood.

He took it for granted that his big unwashed balls must've smelled sweet as chocolate.

And you felt this complete lack of self-reflection made him as much like some animated meat in the world as a man.

And you liked that about him.

It was exactly this quality that elevated him to such a state of perfected masculinity.

He would never pause for even a second, even if he was uncertain of his next required action.

His pace would never fail to fall in synch with the scamper and breeze of the forest, the drift of the West's wide open or the multi-planed acute rushes of the unrelenting city.

Like a thick, throbbing five-foot-six penis on two feet, a collar cinching under its head, his mellow bump through the world stood up noticeably and cracked a smile only when noticing this same walking-genital quality in someone else.

And then he would smile, because for him, this recognition was a liberty granted: his fundamental simplicity justified.

*

42

James told Dennis to turn off the radio. – *It just gets in the way.*

You scooted behind James in the backseat and squeezed his shoulders.

Recoiling, he glanced at Dennis and told you that he likes the tension in his neck.

He's not going to stop even to eat.

He said he's – *Gonna keep the hunger on.*

Both men stared straight ahead.

You wondered what it was that any of you was projecting on to the road.

It wasn't some *Freedom.*

You were all three too tied to the road to romanticize it like that.

And you always carried condoms with you.

That was the one discipline that you never let slide.

With a dull ache in your abdomen, you kept an eye on them and they never glanced back at you.

You reached down and stuffed a sock down into your panties.

*

You sang to yourself in the backseat, and neither of the guys seemed to notice or mind.

You'd driven a long way the day before to get to Santa Fe, but it never occurred to you and you never got the impression that you were particularly in a hurry.

You had no idea or expectation either way about heading out on the road the next day, continuing east or not.

Having witnessed the car sprint the night before, you assumed that these guys drifted from sprint to sprint, following hunches or whims in no particular hurry, a meditation on America.

It never occurred to you that in between sprints, they were in some kind of marathon and that this marathon that you hadn't even realized was happening in the background too big to be seen, somehow grounded everything.

The marathon's course unified the car and James's mind and Dennis's body all into pure drive.

The sprints, it turned out, were only possible because they existed within the marathon.

And the marathon itself, though meaningless, granted some semblance of meaning to its participants.

*

The experience of travel, the drift: people don't think about it, but sleeping anywhere, whenever, that's the lesson travel really teaches.

Life without pattern.

Eight-hours-a-night sleep and sixteen hours waking, that's an exception.

It changes you to be up for two hours and then sleep for one, over and over through each twenty-four hour cycle.

It has the cumulative effect of living a fifty-sum-day-week, each morning's alarm and each night's last call separated by no more than the shock awake into some sudden small town or rest stop, and the stumble to the next quiet spot.

Sleep under a chipped-paint table in the back room of a café for an hour; or sleep leaning cheek to hot glass sitting up shotgun in a parked car; sleep in the shade of a statue in the park.

Driving, the only continuity.

And maybe you'd grown immune to the smell of oil.

The car had come to smell sweet, like your three bodies combined, like overripe nectarines.

*

Pulling into Boswell around dawn, the white noise and blur of the rain so severe, you didn't know how long you'd slept for.

Boswell what? Arkansas? Oklahoma?

The slam of the car door woke you, surprised to find yourself in the unfamiliar car – a GTO.

His shoulders hunched, Dennis shuffled away from the car.

He'd been driving while you slept shotgun.

And your neck cramped from the weight of how your head had hung.

You were parked behind The 55 in front of a gas station under a small covering not large enough for the GTO to also fit under.

Warren stood out front, the gas station not yet open.

Stuck in the rain, bouncing on his toes, he greeted Dennis – *The men's room is locked.*

Dennis shrugged and blew into his cupped hands.

With light steps through the rain, lifting his knees high to keep his fancy boots from the mud, Warren jogged over to the other side of the building to check for another restroom.

*

Dennis had looked under the hood of Warren's GTO on the side of the road the night before.

The rain had died down for a bit and, sharing hard-boiled eggs and scotch, Dennis performed the check-up in the beams of The 55.

He diagnosed that the GTO needed some repair and agreed that you'd all wait with Warren in Boswell.

You figured you must've been up the whole night.

The dense rattle of the rain swaddling your thoughts so tightly, you felt awake within a dream.

You could hardly breathe with the need to stretch, move, walk.

But the rain, near blinding and immersively loud, kept you seated shotgun: stretching your neck, tapping your knees.

Inhaling deep, you lift your chest and hold it, hold it.

And exhaling hard, your chest falling slowly, you mimicked sleep's breath.

But the superficial prompt couldn't stifle your restlessness.

Across the driveway, the abandoned bench of a truck's backseat left out in the rain was soaking.

The garage door was left flipped up, tools in plain sight.

Dennis would've known what to do with them.

You wouldn't know where to sell them.

And finding the second restroom also locked, pulling at the door and cursing, Warren turned and peed on the side of the garage, one arm flung over his head against the building's gutter overflowing down on him.

*

Warren was older, probably even over forty, older than some of your friends' parents.

He dressed particularly: a tight sweater over a butterfly collar and tight chinos.

You thought that he must be rich.

Seen through wet glass at daybreak, his face – features puffy, a big shiny white overbite – you knew it was in your head, some hypnosis of sleeplessness and the drone of loud rain, but his face *seemed* warped like the view at the corners of a fish-tank, disproportioned and cubed against its curves.

Dennis ducked into the backseat of The 55 and dug through the toolbox.

Screwdriver in hand, he jogged across the street.

Turning back around after zipping up, curious, Warren ran along behind him.

You needed to pee badly too, but were apprehensive about crouching in some wet bush in the cold.

And you didn't feel like putting on a show, or pulling a wadded up bloody sock from out of your pants.

Down on one knee in the mud at the back of an abandoned car across the street, Dennis removed the license plate with a few quick, efficient gestures.

Warren stood over him watching, his posture taut and shivering in cold rain.

You really just wanted to fall back asleep while waiting for the gas station to open, but you knew that needing to pee so badly, you'd never be able to.

Your chill was so severe, it made the need to pee even worse, but also made you dread stepping out to pee even more.

Finally you had no choice.

Mustering your will, you stepped out, took a couple long steps and crouched between piles of wet tires.

You balanced yourself with one hand up against a rusted bathtub thrown up in a bush and discarded at a sloping angle.

How you would've loved a bath then, not just to warm up, but for time alone.

Your muscles might actually unclench.

Dennis and Warren trotted back across the street, hunched against the cold, eyes down against the rain.

Neither of them noticed you.

You dug the bloody sock down into the mud under the bushes.

Dennis crouched at the back of The 55 and quickly replaced its plate with the one he'd nabbed across the street.

You guessed that maybe Dennis must've owned The 55.

So strange, that shared responsibility: the car, the only possession either of the guys seemed to have.

*

That bathtub thrown up into the bush that you had leaned against, tilted a little and gave way under your weight when you started to stand.

You fantasized for a second about flipping it and letting the rain fill it up.

Freezing, you were about to jump back into the GTO

But at that moment Warren walked over to The GTO, grabbed his flask from the trunk, and got in the driver's seat.

You didn't have it in you to nod along to one of his ridiculous monologues. – *I get to one side of this country and I just bounce right back across like a rubber ball.*

– *Hard pull, zero to sixty in seven-point-five.*

You just wanted, just needed to sleep.

Warren emptied his flask in one long pull.

He didn't blink.

He looked terrified of the horizon.

You hesitated, lingering between the piles of tires and the wet bushes.

You liked the idea that our moods serve to help us distinguish ourselves from World.

The shadows lightened on the small town main street in the early morning rain.

You didn't know where you were: Oklahoma? Arkansas? And *this guy*?

You'd jumped in with those two, James and Dennis.

Jumped in the souped-up, optimized-by-way-of-reduction '55 Chevy in Flagstaff.

This geezer Warren in his GTO appeared out of nowhere with his stupid dare to race.

Out of nowhere, as everyone always does or everyone always has.

Long Island to San Francisco, you thought, and back again and again.

*

With a deep sigh, Warren stepped out of the car and returned to his trunk to grab another bottle.

James emerged from the driver's seat of The 55.

His stringy hair stuck to his face in the rain.

Trotting like a deer, he peeled his light shirt, now wet, away from his ribs.

He approached Warren, who was standing at the open trunk.

– *You seen her around?*

Warren looked confused. – *Who?*

The girl, you know, Bird, whatever her name is.

No. – Warren shook his head and looked irritated to be asked something so inconsequential compared to the troubling issues on his mind.

– *You know where I can get a plate? I don't wanna be left out in the cold, you know what I mean? I don't wanna be from out of state.*

James turned and hands on hips, his focus concentrated

and distant, he looked around.

You ducked down a little between the tires and the wet bush.

He didn't see you.

Warren got back in his car.

Sitting up straight, he tilted the bottle that he'd pulled from the trunk to refill his flask, careful not to spill it in his lap.

He dropped the now-empty bottle in front of the passenger seat, and took another steep pull from the flask.

*

You watched James march off into the old downtown, looking for you.

With drooped shoulders and his head hanging, bashful about his height and his hair always in his eyes, he had a way of moving in quick, tiny stutters.

While his shoulders slid smooth along a plane, the rest of his humped posture bounced.

Like laundry hung in a man-approximation and sent on casts down the line, he looked like a scarecrow with an appointment to make.

So you understood the bad first impressions James always seemed to make.

Seemed no one ever met him and took any kind of instant liking to him or even treated him friendly.

He had a way that triggered people's suspicions quick.

Even Warren, immediately obnoxious as his constant bragging was, it was obvious that he had receded completely into the folds of his bruised ego, you couldn't fault Warren for his overcompensating.

But against James, people's defenses went up as soon as he appeared.

It could be just the shadowed recesses of his eyes under those severe brows.

He was certainly the only person you'd ever met that upon first meeting you thought – "Wow, what an intense skeleton he must have."

Seemed everyone he met had his or her own unique variation of that response, and that was enough to put everyone on defense.

And it didn't help: that dry skin of his.

His chapping, pale and layered, it made you itch just to look at him.

But mostly, honestly, it was that stare.

*

James looked at people as if he was trying to project his own mind into the skull of the person he spoke to.

You knew it when he was attempting to do it to you, so it didn't work.

But you recognized the shift in his focus.

The dilation in his eyes was a real material shift, however contrived the fixing of his stare may've seemed.

When you'd been the focus of it, you squirmed, wanted to shout – *Just drop it. OK? It doesn't work.*

And of course even as you wiggled out of it, he'd insist that he had no idea what you were talking about.

But you knew better.

You too had a stare, and you too kept your hair in your eyes to hide it.

You knew when you were turning it on or off, so you knew that he knew too.

In those couple days, you'd already witnessed his stare a few times, and it was the worst when you stood as a third party witness to it.

Because when you watched him doing it to someone else, then, from the outside you could see what was actually happening and how it really would – *should* even, *couldn't help but* – work.

Not the mechanics of it, you didn't see that – laserbeams or anything.

But it was equally as real.

His eyes, projectors as much as receptor-cones, did shoot when focused with specific aim, especially if the person on the receiving end was vulnerable, open to it.

His mind, like a beam received, could – should, couldn't help but – fill the skull of the other person like smoke, first finding the furthest parameters and outlining for itself how far it could extend, then increasing not in range, but in density within the established space of the hosting skull.

And in that way James attempted to throw his own mind like a ventriloquist into the heads of those he met.

Only thing was, he just wasn't good at it.

He could do it a little bit, and did, and that was something. But you'd never seen anyone fall for it.

He never approached anyone or started conversations.

But people along the way, roadside or in some small towns, people would be friendly.

An auctioneer in an old plaid suit, an old man with a greasy scalp, counting out his pennies, or teenagers in bikinis at the lake-side beach with cans of beer, anyone – everyone James came across, five seconds or less into conversation with him ended up shaking their heads.

Looking away, rattled and annoyed, no one could name exactly why they were all so impatient to end any conversation with him.

And James would shrug and saunter off.

He'd have to wait to meet that whoever, that anyone, susceptible to his mind-operations.

A failed Rasputin, he drove and drove.

You imagined he must've thought the road a beam his own gaze projected ahead of The 55 to skate along.

*

James did have a nice smile, actually, though it appeared only when he had the good sense to laugh at himself.

For other people, his thin lips remained reserved mostly for minor scorn.

His generally passive sense of himself in the world remained aloof.

But, like daylight seeping through the cracks between

boards in an old swamp shack, he did, Thank God, laugh at himself easily enough, aware of his inability to even smile about anything else.

Nothing else was meaningful enough to him to actually be funny.

And this self-awareness must've been at least some minor variation of charm.

Dennis on the other hand, his simple utility, his pure gendering, was the sum of his attractive qualities.

Of course you understood such an attraction contradicted any true potential Dennis and you could ever have for any meaningful connection.

But he did make you laugh when you'd have a moment alone.

Playful, he'd act out ironic romantic promises or big gestures of affection, a squeeze of your hand after ignoring you all day, a hand to your lower back as you passed through a doorway, always with a cynical smirk.

Like a wink – *Isn't it pretty to think so?*

*

At that gas station that morning in the rain in Boswell, James acted like your babysitter or your boss, heading off on a mission to hunt you down.

You were just about to get back into one of the cars.

You thought maybe Warren would have a razor you could borrow.

But then you overheard their conversation, and James's tone of voice with Warren.

And you saw that stare that he planned to keep aimed right on you.

As much as you didn't like the look of that town, as much as the little roads shooting from it did not appear promising, you knew you had to split.

You didn't want to get back into either of those cars with any of those three.

You dreaded equally: James's stare, Warren's hammy

stories, and Dennis's confidence, each a variation of attempting to pin you down.

Dennis was sound asleep, a snoring pile thrown back on the bench in front of the gas station.

In the GTO, Warren looked straight ahead off into the distance, unblinking.

No one was watching, so you didn't say anything.

You weren't sneaking off, but it didn't seem necessary to announce your departure.

The rain relaxed into a drizzle.

You seized your opportunity.

*

You grabbed your bag from the backseat of The 55 and started off in the opposite direction from where James had headed, quickly cutting over a block so he wouldn't see you if he circled back.

Tired as you were, dazed even, it still felt good to walk, to work out the cramps in your legs and your neck.

The morning air felt cool, refreshing.

Kicked you awake a little.

And that familiar rush of heading towards whatever happened to happen next, that thrill overtook your exhaustion.

*

But Boswell's decay had no charm to it.

Two empty buildings stood side by side, but most of the buildings were set far apart from each other.

People did live in these little buildings, and their lives, their symmetrical senses, opposable thumbs, and numbing loneliness were just like your own.

But that confidence the white steeples and TV antennas pinpricking the distance gave them, a confidence they couldn't even recognize that they possessed, that must've made their minds different enough from yours.

How could they not be a different species?

The sun came out in wide beams, cutting bright through the drizzling gray, and making all that peeling, glistening wet paint look eerie.

Every surface in the town – fences, garages, abandoned storefronts – curled up to reveal the colors, the layers of painted-over pasts hidden underneath.

You didn't like it at all.

You didn't like that town in Oklahoma or Arkansas, Boswell, or wherever one bit.

You didn't see anyone.

Not a single person moved about, but you still knew what everyone in that town must've looked like, every one of them: big glasses with glares hiding their eyes, gap-toothed and missing teeth, thin greasy hair.

No thank you.

You didn't need it.

You didn't need their crummy spilled-Coke-sticky-puddle-ant-trap-powder-poison of a town one bit.

You considered turning back and at least sticking with those guys long enough to make it out of town.

*

Warren, like some stupid, rugged character-actor from a hundred Westerns, he said things like – *You know I'm not afraid of winning this thing and taking that car from you.*

And James, perpetually sighing like some kind of arrogant balladeer proud of his turn of phrase, would keep his cool and respond simply – *Well, I'm not afraid of you winning either, man.*

And Dennis, always on the cusp of a smile like some ditzy beach bum, would nod.

You had to get away from those guys.

Boswell Lanes, Boswell State Bank.

The rain had died down almost completely.

Your big army bag slung over your shoulder, you walked off through the few blocks of the old downtown.

Early, nothing had opened yet.

On a brick building with a screen door, the screen door reflecting pale yellow on the slick pavement, old posters crinkled in the tapping rain.

Daylight thunder boomed as you looked over an abandoned theater, its marquees empty except for tangles of dust blanketing burnt-out bulbs.

Two old men swept the sidewalk in front of the café next to the feed store.

*

Not far out from downtown at all, past the last rusty trailers, the pavement ended.

You trudged on, the gloppy mud unavoidable, the sun beating.

You wondered if anyone from the city can ever see bales of hay and think of anything besides their own impression of how the light changes on them over the course of a day.

Further on but not much further, you passed the last of the splintering telephone poles.

You considered turning back for real.

Endless fences on both sides; one small section on the left had been repaired and looked newer than the rest of the wire.

Near a dried-up pond, train tracks were bent up mangled.

The sun hot and high, it might end up early afternoon by the time you could stick your thumb up for a passing jalopy.

But you kept walking.

In the distance, faintly, an engine, and you thought for a second, hoped, it might be The 55.

Maybe James had come to find you.

But it wasn't.

Just some farm machinery way off in the fields, couldn't even see it.

Wanting to collapse, needing sleep so badly, you walked on.

The heat started wearing you down.

Such muscle atrophy, you couldn't shake images of boiled

meat falling from bone.

Recognizing no advantage in succumbing to this image, you kept on without accepting it, replacing it instead with a conscious blockade in place.

You visualized a wall wrapping around your head, keeping out all fear, all dust and heat, and harnessed the fight to stagger on.

But the dust – or maybe it was pollen, as all the dirt was mud, but something was in the air and it tickled the back of your throat.

The sustained feeling of being about to sneeze, and never sneezing.

Some dryness hung in the air, this grit like a swarming itch waiting only for you to stumble into it.

Deep thirst and the choking: that was enough.

You had to admit that you'd gotten yourself into some new kind of mess and once again, had no one to blame at all, but yourself.

Shit.

You had done something stupid.

You flopped down, cross-legged on the shoulder of the road, wiped out.

Nauseous with the need to sleep, your muscles clenched in defense, your head pounding with the charge of exhaustion, your neck, you moved to sit on the purple stump of a tree.

It felt petrified and its thick roots were knotted like lint.

Thought you heard the growl of The 55 in the distance again, but it never approached.

Far off in the fields, a siren was tall above a tower.

*

Sustained travel with no ends except for the travel itself, really did essentially amount to nothing more than the constant battle against one's own sleeping patterns.

Using your bag as a pillow, that same smudged bag that you'd thrown on the ground of puddled public restrooms, you'd sleep, your arm thrown over your face to block out the light.

Every nap lasted as long as the circumstances of the opportunity allowed.

The rare full night's sleep would throw the whole next day off.

How many continuous hours awake is a full day supposed to be?

Traveling partners afforded this to each other: two hours for you here, on the bench behind that building, on your back, knees lifted, then I get a shaded hour here in the grass.

Partnered, any moment without direct sensory stimulus you could tilt over.

But alone, you had to keep your own lookout.

*

Finally, you found yourself immersed so you had no choice but to accept it.

The familiar long hours of silent staring: strung-out and jittery, cramping along your ribs and your shoulders clenched, your peripheral vision slimming and your stare locked into hard.

Yourself in the world, always somewhere and always the same: somewhere new, and hunger.

Awake in the dream, a big part of it, that feeling of waking up somewhere new, the roar of the road leveling all the landscapes that you zoomed through into a sustained hum with minor bumps, that singular experience – no present.

No present: there was only the mulling over of the past or the resolve, it felt so real in the moment, of exactly how differently you'd live your life when you had the chance to return to it – *if* you ever could really arrive somewhere.

Thing was though – the big question, once the dream-state and that sense of no-present had been going on so long that you couldn't even remember the other side of it – how did you know when it was time to return to your life?

You didn't know when it had even begun, the dream-state and that sense of no-present.

So many cars you'd ducked in and out of, so many strange men, the hammy pinky-meat of each of their little fists clenching the wheel.

There was the persistent sense that the dream-state of the drift was not real life.

Your real life was something to be returned to, eventually, when you knew all at once that the time was right, the time had come to snap your gaze from the hypnosis of the yellow stripe of the lane in the beams.

Was it a childish dream to imagine maybe James would come bumping down this road to find you, save you, bring you anywhere?

And what about when the dream-state itself seems to have become real life?

*

From your bag you took out your small collection of photos and articles that you'd cut from magazines: Mick Jagger shirtless in a long scarf, Paul Newman brooding in a gray crewneck.

Since you were a little girl, you'd always been fixated on glamour.

Maybe the exceptionalism of the stars seemed like a positive version of your own alienation.

If you could achieve that lifestyle someday, maybe your own isolation would be pacified.

On the flipside of a photo of dead-eyed Jim Morrison was a strange picture that you'd never noticed before.

You couldn't make out what the mechanical maze-like form was.

There were two complete sentences, two possible captions.

But the way that the piece had been cut from the paper, you couldn't determine which caption described the photo.

Either: *The Intel Corporation's first commercially viable 'microprocessor.'*

Or: *After a record-breaking twenty-four days in space, three Russians cosmonauts were killed when their capsule depressurized during their descent.*

*

It reminded you.

You remembered the crackling sputter of a newscast when you were a kid.

– *'I see the earth. It is so beautiful.'*

– *These were the first words ever spoken from a man in space when Russian cosmonaut Yuri Gagarin made history today at the age of twenty-seven.*

– *His spaceship, the Vostok One, orbited the earth for eighty-nine-and-a-half minutes.*

You never forgot those words: I see the earth. It is so beautiful.

Except for the hair pulled back from your forehead, by 1961, by the time you were eight years old in Long Island, you already looked exactly the same.

Your stare had already developed by then, your perfect blankness.

But you hadn't yet figured out how to best harness its power.

At twenty-five-years-old, your mom already looked tired, tired in the most expansive sense of the word.

She looked like you, like you would grow up to look: same small frame, same thick, wavy red hair.

But the same pale coloring on her, your same features on her face, that same face on her head, it all needed some smoothing at the edges, like she was you under a crinkling plastic, or a flower petal cut from rough canvas.

Your little brother would've been six then.

With his Naval Academy fade, his head looked big like a wobbling lollipop on his brittle, stick frame.

– *When asked why Mr. Gagarin had been chosen for this distinction, his instructors described him as 'very difficult, if not impossible to upset.'*

– *An old woman, her granddaughter, and a cow were the first witnesses.*

The wallpaper peeled above the stove.

The radiator's high whistle, almost silent, seemed to emanate from exactly that spot.

If your mom was twenty-five then, then your dad would've been about forty-seven.

Coarse hair sprouting from his ears and nose, he was jagged as a junkyard, an iceberg of a man, squeezing out at the seams of a suit two sizes too small.

*

Sitting out along that road on your own, you would've been happy to see your dad.

Or your brother.

As soon as that gas station opened so Warren could get his repair, James and Dennis planned to take off and find the nearest track.

And then you would never find them again.

And they'd never find you out along that road.

And who else would ever get you out of there – Boswell, wherever?

By early afternoon, noon even, those two would be a hundred miles away, walking the hot parking lot of some track, kicking tires with all the other guys, all looking under each other's hoods, all confident and guarded.

Speaking coy, speaking in code, that's how the races were set up and run.

Dennis and James loved their codes hidden out in the open.

Not just the simplicity of the patches stitched on jackets and the bandanas hung from which pocket and folded how, but the functional necessities were especially primed for coding.

Some rims spun better on a particular sized wheel, but were only for flash on a smaller wheel.

How much had been pared down, stripped from the dash?

This was all recognizable at a glance if you knew what to look for.

LET GO AND GO ON AND ON

They loved how wrong someone like Warren was, wrong about every possible small choice, and how being wrong excluded him from everything that he longed to identify with.

And as much as the codes were all set up to exclude him, more than that they were rites of passage: knowledge gained and experience, instant respect shared in affirmative nods when coming across someone else who'd known to do it all correctly, someone else who got it.

*

You always remembered those words: I see the earth. It is so beautiful.

And maybe you were losing your cool.

If you didn't focus on anything specifically, the fields were the color of singed cheese.

You probably hadn't been out there more than a few minutes, but lugging around your own exhaustion, you just didn't have the surplus energy to keep the panic away.

You felt it coming on again.

You had done something stupid.

No one would come down that road.

And even if someone did, you'd never want to get in a car with him.

It wouldn't be your dad or your brother, bouncing up to lend a hand to the sloppy model far from home.

Walking off had been a real stupid idea.

James and Dennis would just say *Oh well* and find a track and be off, and that'd be that.

*

Maybe you could've walked back to the gas station and waited with Warren for his repair.

But they said it'd be simple and not take long at all.

He'd probably be gone already.

Warren didn't even realize that James and Dennis finding a track while he got the repair was their way of giving him the head start he was too proud to accept.

By the time you got back to the gas station, if you could summon the energy to carry yourself there, Warren would probably already be stopping along some other country road outside of town, picking up some hitchhiking cowboy-businessman.

– *How far you goin'?*

– *Oh. Just gotta get up on over to Lil' Rock.*

Unless you were already past Little Rock, which you might've been, but you really thought you must've been in just about Oklahoma.

And Warren, he just couldn't help himself – *Yep. Goin' straight through there on my way to Virginia. CIA Headquarters. I have these papers to deliver. Top Secret.*

Thing was, Warren believed his own bullshit so deeply that it might've all been true, in a way.

He seemed to report the world exactly as he saw it, best he could.

His storytelling and truth stretching rarely, if ever, seemed malicious.

Maybe he could only speak poetically, his metaphorical truths never impeded on by facts.

But still Warren was exhausting, undeniably, maybe more so than anyone you'd ever met, even if you could get past blaming or resenting him.

His practiced speech about the GTO – *hard pull, zero to sixty in seven-point-five.*

His tone clunky and his pathetic gaze worried, you doubted he knew what his words were supposed to mean any more than you did.

*

James and Dennis would be walking some parking lot in silence, as silently as they drove, the hum of the track's crowd in the distance no different than the whir of the road.

And after a while they'd negotiate with some yokels, try to psyche them out with mind-games and James's stare.

Each taking one side, choreographed symmetrically, they'd flip the hood open from its hinge at the front of the car, lift it off, and set it aside.

Their unified front, their telepathy: it was such a practiced performance, a demonstration of militancy.

But you knew that it'd take no more than one of them betting the tools.

The other one would have to be aware to not let his chin drop.

One impulsive, proud bet would reveal the fraud of their partnership, the enabling pretenses, unspoken, the wink implied between *all* partners, qualifying: partners – *for now*.

And maybe after a little while you would be able to get up from that tree stump on the side of the road and keep on walking.

Maybe you'd be lucky enough to find another tree stump to sit on by dusk, pull your hair through the hours, another night on defense, waiting for a car to pass, terrified of any beams that might appear.

Were you somehow lonely without those guys?

You were tough, or you were trapped?

One thing, you sure hadn't had to fight off so many zits in a real long time.

It gets hard to keep your face clean traveling, the way dust sticks to sweat.

*

At school when you were a kid, all the desks were arranged on the cracked, old tiles in a wide half-moon.

The teacher, a middle-aged woman in layers of polyester, her glasses low on her nose, sat in the middle and read out loud to the surrounding children.

All the other kids huddled up next to her in the closest seats, cross-legged at her feet or hunched under desks.

Some stood behind her, some sucking their thumbs.

Some girls braided each other's hair.

And, eyes closed, some kids scratching each other's backs

simultaneously, they were all always totally absorbed in her stories.

But across the room, behind a beam that allowed the teacher the pretense of pretending to not see you, you would sit alone, absorbed in your own books, reading quietly to yourself.

You thought about that beam, how you and the teacher both played along that neither of you could see the other, and how that beam allowed you to do so.

*

Dee Dee was your true friend.

Your lockers were next to each other first day of high school, assigned alphabetically.

And you were seated next to each other in a couple classes.

She was easy to talk to, snarky and rude, judgmental of everyone except you.

She was a head shorter than you, and wide.

None of the boys ever noticed her, but that never prevented her from having opinions about whose advances you should accept or reject.

She cherished her role as your advisor, and though she had a good number of other friends besides you, you didn't really know any of them.

And she always chose you over them.

You didn't think about her much.

When you did think about her, you were always mad that she just couldn't understand why you had to leave.

A couple times, the last time especially, you tried to explain very carefully, best you could, why you had to leave.

And she just played dumb.

She pretended like none of it made any sense to her, but you knew that she had to understand.

She had just finally turned her judgment on you.

You thought about that sometimes, how you wished that you could call her, when you did occasionally miss her.

But you didn't want to have to try to explain again.

And other than her, there was really just your friend the

other model.

She had stayed in New York, seen the whole program through.

*

And you could see clearly how the whole thing was about to play out for you out there on that country road alone.

Maybe by dusk you might hopefully summon the will to move on to the next tree stump.

And by then Warren would be yammering on to a different cowboy hitchhiker.

– *Hard pull, zero to sixty in seven-point-five.*

He'd show off, make the cowboy squeal – *Hoo-wee!*

– *Yep. That's one thing I learned as a test pilot boy. You can never go fast enough.*

Wow!

– *Yes sir. This stretch of road here between my ranch in Dallas and my beach house in the keys, this stretch of road here …*

And then it'd get dark.

And after dark, standing alone, cool, you knew Dennis would be watching James race a kid in a factory-built Corvette marketed to represent Speed Itself.

All that Corvette kid's hushed friends surrounding him, unable to believe a '55 Chevy could be so optimized, Dennis would be aware not to gloat or even smirk.

Keeping an eye out over his shoulder, waiting for a wrench to come crashing down on his skull, he'd never let on that he even realized he stood alone among a dozen rivals.

With the smell of motor-oil wafting through night air, he'd feel a stir in his bulge.

And what difference would it ever have even made to anyone that you got out of the car, walked off?

You were too impulsive and stupid to hang in there and do no more than the simplest thing necessary to continue, even if, goddamn, sometimes continuing something does seem like the hardest thing in the world to do.

*

But you were saved.

James pulled up hardly half an hour after you'd left the gas station.

He came up on you roadside, slouching halfway between the tree-stump you'd gotten up from and the one in the distance, your destination.

Seeing him approach, you stood up straight, weren't about to let on that maybe you wanted him to give you a ride.

Maybe you'd *let* him give you one.

Neither of you said a word, but you knew that he'd come and find you.

You threw your big army bag in the backseat and stepped in shotgun, tired, relieved.

Not even saying hello, James spread his long arm over the back of your seat and though his chest rose and fell deeply, nostrils flared, he never even turned to look at you.

And you didn't know what the hell was on his mind, with that stupid stare all the time.

His stupid default expression, intense glaring, got weirder the more constant it remained.

Dennis did all the maintenance, day-to-day and emergency, so you guessed that maybe James got some kind of satisfaction just being the driver, which maybe you thought was kind of mysterious or interesting.

Idle, the car knocked its loud, jagged purr.

After pulling away, you still both hadn't spoken a word.

The 55 growled through golden dust and dry corn strange, back past the rusted-out abandoned cars and trailers you'd walked by before.

*

You were laughing together by the time you pulled over to the side of the road to swap seats.

The shared rupture of over-tired silliness startled you both awake.

66

But you knew it was horrible to laugh about that.

The laughter settled.

Running around the back of car, smiling, James tucked in his shirt while trotting, un-tucked it again settling back down shotgun.

Your eyes closed, his hand on yours heavy and warm, he demonstrated shifting the gear positions. – *This is first, here's reverse* ...

Aware of your breath quick and shallow, you said – *Is this a game?*

He inhaled, held it a moment.

Green shoots sprouted up tall all around, taller than The 55.

Not yet – he responded.

Shifting into first, you messed up the clutch and killed the car with a single lurch forward.

I can't do it. – Your voice warbled high in your throat with frustration.

The growling volume of the stationary vehicle quieted all at once, faint smoke hovered.

His stiff movement and lingering pause awkward, his stare, he pulled you over for a kiss hard and sudden.

Submitting to him but slowing him down, trying to help smooth him out, you sighed.

I can *do this.* – You said.

You moved to the backseat together.

Your head thrown back, were you imagining opening your arms wide and tickling your face into the corn?

When could it have been that any one of those stalks had last been touched?

Each was one of many among its like kind.

After leaning on you a couple times, a weak spurt on the front of James's jeans.

Even though they hung from your knee, it still took longer to pull your jeans back on than the act itself had taken.

Silent, James smirked at you and looked away as he tucked his shirt in.

Still, the thought of you with anyone else ...

He climbed out and ran around the back of the car to get back into the driver's seat.

*

But it was good that you made it back to the gas station sooner than later.

Dennis had moved from the bench he'd been sleeping sitting up on over to the driver's seat of the GTO

He slept, leaning his forehead against the window.

It must've been Saturday: kids were playing baseball in the street.

A hillbilly in sleeveless overalls, he had a fade haircut and lurked around the gas station office, held the phone to his ear, but he didn't say anything to you guys.

The hillbilly must've walked up on Warren passed out drunk, down in the dirt at the bumper of the truck parked in the garage, its license plate loosened but still connected.

James shook Dennis awake and you hopped into The 55.

The cops rolled up.

James and Dennis, before the cops even had a chance to address them, pulled Warren back to the GTO, each grabbing him under an arm, his fancy boots dragging.

They dropped him still asleep, shotgun in his own car.

Dennis driving The 55 and James driving the GTO, pulled off.

The cops followed for a block or two before James and Dennis, with a quickly shouted plan at a fork in the road, split up so the cops had to choose which car to follow.

James stopped to pick up a Carburetor Rebuild kit for a 1970 GTO

Meeting back up on the dirt road south of town, the tree stump you'd been sitting on visible in the distance, Dennis did the repair next to a horse that you hadn't noticed before.

The corn was hard sunshine itself blooming, a brightness and life unlike the trawl of lived experience, its endless lumps and tangles and letdowns.

Other people often weren't very interesting to you.

But then when they sometimes were, it was even worse.

It made you nervous.

After Dennis finished, the three of you pulled off in The 55, leaving Warren asleep shotgun in his own car.

*

Back in the car and resolved to driving again, it was a relief to return to the familiar waking dream, that drive that you had walked away from: the yellow stripe of the lanes in the beams.

Being unable to sleep, anywhere, never; eventually that changes you, changes your mind.

But you'd been preparing for that even before traveling.

Back in New York, before you left to begin your drift, every day happened the same.

You'd close the last bar and in the morning you'd wake up startled at first light, reviewing the previous night's misdeeds, transgressions of empathy, and social affronts.

The review always involved your hypocrisy, how you treated other people.

Shocked to realize what a horrible person you actually were.

Every morning you felt terrible, sick with guilt, like the sun rose only to stand judgment on your late night behavior.

You flattered yourself a Good Person, kind and considerate.

This flattery enabled you through your dull afternoons, usually high and internalized.

And then drinks, usually around dark, starting a little before, and the depressants would saturate your attention the same as the darkness saturated the daylight.

And it'd be tilting through those hours that you might be around anyone or start talking at all.

And so if you insisted on flattering yourself a Good Person, so kind and considerate in the afternoons on your own, in your head, of course you had to actually *be* a Good Person later.

But you knew that you weren't.

Intellectually, sometimes you thought other people made you so nervous because you just loved them so much that you could never be good enough for them, and so you had to have a couple drinks.

But you'd always been purposefully distant.

You knew that.

You kept peoples' approaches short.

It was simple.

You'd figured that out.

You said polite things.

You always said the right thing.

But the timing told the truth.

The pauses, the bumps and stumbles of your speech patterns couldn't hide the struggle you faced: the great effort you had to put into saying the polite thing, the right thing.

Your impulse, if you didn't work to say the right thing, was just always to make up silly stories: a domesticated coyote you kept as a pet in the city, your private island you needed the spare change to move to.

You'd fallen into the habit of asking everyone for spare change without even realizing you'd done so.

Didn't matter how supposedly close you might've been to someone.

You would be like that: purposefully distant, with whatever new boy might've been around a couple hours each day for weeks.

And then, even if you didn't see him for some days and thought that you missed him, it still happened when you'd see him again.

People that you'd known your entire life, that's how you ended up being towards everyone.

But that guilt at first light, this was how it always happened: you'd wake up startled, realizing that you had rushed some acquaintance you'd run into at one of the bars or on the street.

A fireman, the older son of neighbors back in Long Island, you were six years old when you met him and still somehow you'd run into him at least weekly, ever since moving to the city.

And he was always all-smiles, even though you never didn't rush him.

Couldn't he tell?

And yes, the bubbly pontifications he was always so eager to share were irritating. – *I've figured it out. Everyone here is a little crazy. That's what this scene, this circle, that's what's happening here, how we've all found each other.*

Wow, you thought, keen analysis, Einstein.

But still, did he deserve your hurrying?

Or your building's handyman out alone in a sharp coat, shouting over a crowd for the hundredth time exactly how to wiggle the basement key.

No one deserved to be hurried.

But you always just had to split.

Getting away from these guys, it swelled up inside you, urgent.

It was no choice, just an inevitability, as inevitable as you waking shocked at dawn, stunned with self-loathing and regret, shocked by your own hypocrisy, to realize that you were not actually a Good Person.

Back in The 55, resolved to driving again, everything simple again, you were relieved to return to the familiar waking dream, that drive you had walked away from.

You would get some sleep.

Needed to catch up quick, build a surplus.

Still, you knew you'd have to get out somewhere before they got back to the coast.

You'd left New York not knowing for certain where you were heading, or when you might eventually stop moving.

But you did know that you had no intention of ending up back there.

You were never one to romanticize your own confusion.

You only liked The Rolling Stones because of the black streak running through all their songs.

So it was only common sense to you, not Romance or Freedom, to be heading West, in the same direction the sun moves across the sky, the direction one heads towards the end of things.

*

You got a lot of work when you first arrived in Manhattan, only the year before.

In 1970 you were sixteen, feeling bashful and clumsy modeling a short coat with a fur-lined collar under hot lights.

You'd stand in perfect stoic profile until called to snap into action.

Pout and coo for the camera, kick one long leg out to show off a knee-high boot.

The photographer you worked with a lot, his hairline receding though he must've been only in his early thirties, dressed up too self-consciously cool to fool anyone.

You'd seen *Blowup* at The Cinema One, so you always felt a little embarrassed for him.

He truly thought no one would recognize how hard he was trying to be David Hemmings?

– *Beautiful, beautiful. La-la-la.*

He responded to your every flutter and bend with flattery.

– *That's it, just like that. Blow me a kiss honey. La-dee-dee-da.*

– *That's it. There's the attitude, let's see more of that. Give it to me. La-dee-da-da-dee-da.*

Floating a moment, you moved in half-time to the photographer's wild waves.

The frantic sycophants and assistants were unified in the strobe of flashing bulbs.

– *Shoulder up baby. Eyes over here. Look at my hand. Beautiful. Beautiful.*

You followed his instructions but never responded verbally.

Especially dressed up glamorous, being the center of attention, your own voice buried low in your chest, muffled by your throat.

You were still self-conscious about your voice back then.

You saw people's surprise every time you spoke, sometimes even with a look of pity.

Simple as it was, everything about modeling embarrassed

you.

Your friend the other model, dressed identically to you, leaned against the wall.

Whispering in her ear, your modeling coach was pointing out the strengths and weaknesses of your technique.

She, your friend the other model, gave you an encouraging wink.

You slouch? – The photographer throwing his weight to one side, a hand on his hip, looked you up and down.

How tall are you? – He asked.

Five-seven.

Great. – He nodded thoughtfully.

When he smirked, it looked like a wince and made him look even older.

But you liked people that tried to smile and obviously had a hard time of it, more than you liked the easy-smilers.

When he called out – *Isn't she beautiful ladies and gentlemen* – the room snapped to attention and applauded you politely.

You stood, feet spread to shoulder width and mouth agape, winded.

In an instant the room returned to its many tiny conversations.

The photographer called the modeling coach over.

At the catering table, careful to finger only the pieces you would eat, you picked from the serving dishes.

You rolled up cold cuts and, dunking them in a thick onion dip, you'd suck the dip from the end, whistling through the hollow of the rolled meat, then roll it up and dip it again.

Your friend the other model puffed on a joint and offered it to you.

You held it a moment while you finished swishing onion dip in your cheek.

You took a hit, the smoke filling your lungs, burning felt good, and offered it to the photographer with a hand signal.

He made a slouching, humbled show of being tempted. – *Oh I wish I could. I've been getting too paranoid.*

You nodded and exhaled a big cloud of smoke.

There's some CIA shit going around or something. – He said.

You told the photographer – *Last night I set my alarm for the lunar eclipse, but I didn't really even need to because I was so excited about it I never fell asleep. I just watched the clock and got up and got dressed, and then sat and waited for the alarm to go off before I headed outside.*

Yeah?

But I couldn't see anything.

You looked him over closely, up and down.

You stepped to one side and the other, looking him up and down.

He squirmed as you inspected him.

You asked him if he had any spare change.

Unfolding a bill for you, he looked confused.

You explained about your private island, explained you were saving up.

*

As little as you knew her, your friend the other model, you were as close to her as anyone else.

She told tumbling monologues about her family.

Her daddy had oppressive expectations.

And Mommy drank on top of Valium.

There were many nights wandering to track Mommy down.

As a ten-year-old walking her bicycle to look for a passed-out shape in the shadows, she was known by name in every tavern of their exclusive little New England hamlet, its winding streets lined with tall stone walls.

Speaking too loudly in the country club dining room was shameful.

Her siblings and every neighbor had a high-power success story.

She felt the pressure.

You couldn't relate.

So your little game you made up, you'd change the story of

your family every time you answered a question about them with a terse response.

That seemed much simpler.

– *That one died.*

– *No, that one did.*

No one, not even your friend the other model, ever seemed to catch on.

*

You were all stretching in your seats in an Arkansas diner when Warren caught back up to you and stormed up to the table, furious.

Maybe he felt you'd all ditched him, though when racing it had to be expected that one car would pull ahead of the other.

Gruff, he asked Dennis if the leak was fixed in the GTO.

He asked this without at all acknowledging that Dennis had done him a favor, as if this repair was somehow Dennis's responsibility.

You drifted through the room towards the pinball machine.

A sign hung next to it: No Dancing.

You stopped suppressing the urge to sing.

In 1971, traveling, *Satisfaction*, that song was always in your head.

Not like you just hummed the tune a lot, but like it broadcast from your skull.

Dazed with exhaustion and the long heat of a Southern afternoon, you'd fallen silent all day until the song emerged from you as a hum in the backseat, your breath quieter than the whir of the road.

Only after you'd hummed through it continuously for quite a few miles, obscuring any sense of beginning or end, did any of the words begin to form.

Then the guys pulled over to eat.

And it wasn't just uniquely in your head, so maybe it was more like the song was the water that you as a fish swam through.

It hung in the air, everywhere, over everything, like everyone moved through it.

Any time anyone would sing it to themselves, most often not even noticing that they were doing so, no one else would notice that they were singing it either, because it was always just there in the background on a jukebox or someone's humming.

Didn't matter if you could locate its specific source at any moment.

Everyone assumed it would always just be there.

Sashaying through the room, you were singing it, singing with no intention or effort.

And once you realized you were singing – "it's Me this time" – then you also realized that you could unify the room: James and Dennis and Warren and yourself, and the aggressive bumpkins crowding the place, staring you guys down.

You needed only to allow the projection of the song in your head, that song you knew was the same song in each of their heads too, even the bumpkins.

*

SATISFACTION

When I'm driving in my car and that man comes on the radio, he's telling me more and more about some useless information supposed to fire my imagination. When I'm watching my TV and that man comes on to tell me how white my shirts can be but he can't be a man 'cause he doesn't smoke the same cigarettes as me. When I'm riding round the world and I'm doing this and I'm signing that and I'm trying to make some girl who tells me baby better come back later next week cause you see I'm on a losing streak.

*

Dennis and James had calmed Warren down, and Warren ordered food.

This arrogant blonde small-town-quarterback type – a little guy, cocky in that way only little guys can be, confident that someone else has his back – he came up to the table sweating the guys with his ridiculous golly-gee accent.

He set his jaw crooked to breathe through his mouth, his chin lowered, so he could look up at them with a supposedly intimidating bashful look.

– *My buddies and me been wondering where you all might be from?*

You hated those good-old-boy racist rapist inbred yokel asshole motherfuckers.

They really didn't know how monumentally stupid they sounded?

– *You guys wouldn't be hippies now would you?*

– *That your car?*

Dennis offered his reflexive response – *Just passing through.*

But Warren, did he even notice when he told a story?

Anything except the truth was always on the tip of Warren's tongue.

With a big smile he explained to The Local how James and Dennis were brothers out racing The 55, and you were Dennis's wife and he was their manager: a family affair, wholesome.

Right before that small-town pipsqueak hot shot walked up to the table, Dennis had just told Warren – *We're broke, need to get some competition.*

And they hustled up that race they needed passively, just sitting there, drawing attention simply by being outsiders.

And Warren's story, if not saving the day, at least facilitated the day being saved.

And you did your part – *I can't get no satisfaction.*

The arrogant asshole toad told them that the track was in Carlisle, The Carlisle Lakeland International Raceway.

The creep nodded to Warren before stepping away – *Sure did talk to you.*

And Warren smiled big, loving that he knew what to say to anyone, always perfectly charming – *Sure did see you.*

*

In The 55's rumble, what color is the world through corn at sunset when pink becomes gold and gold green?

And how the rows of low green cutting across the brown appear to run.

Again and again, your head knocked against the roof of the car.

Your palms pressed flat against it to weight yourself down to the seat, you bumped hard through a field of tall grass, suddenly too fast for the terrain.

Bushes rushed alongside you low.

Fooling around with the car behind you, irritating the driver by not letting him pass, James took a turn too fast, and right after a bend there was wreckage in the middle of the road.

You were on top of it only a second after seeing it, two cars standing on end right there in the middle of the road.

James jerked the wheel fast and held it tight, trying to brake in as controlled of a manner as possible.

He did good.

Still, you ran off the road fast through the green field.

When The 55 stopped you jumped out and fell straight to the grass, had to sit, shaken, had to breathe deep.

The guys shouted at you, a continuation of the sudden whirlwind, the jolt of one second to the next – *Are you OK? Are you hurt?*

And over and over, you were shouting – *Just scared. I'm just scared. Just scared. I'm alright.*

Back in the middle of the road, an old man, silent and still, sat next to the flipped sideways bottom of his truck.

He stared at the corpse, a young man with a broken neck, lots of blood from where the bone pierced skin, too fresh to have even begun coagulating.

You thought there was no end to the surprises of the human form's potential.

And how red red can get.

And the old man kept calling the corpse "a goddamn fool."
– *You Goddamn Fool.*

Only when the dead body's family pulled up in a station wagon – a young woman with a whole litter of children, all under the age of five or six – she stepped from the car and started to trot and then shout and then jog and then howl and then run and then scream.

And only then did you all return to The 55 off crooked in the field.

*

You drove alongside a truck pulling a long flat trailer behind it.

The trailer was empty and made of planks so it looked like a raft.

After DC we can head down to Florida. – James said.

You didn't say anything.

Dennis said – *Gotta check the points, valves, jets, carbs.*

You began to understand, or at least suspect that James could like you or express interest in you only because you'd already slept with Dennis.

That's what that night in Santa Fe had been about, James walking off.

Dennis must've owned the car.

*

GIMME SHELTER
A storm is threatening my very life today.
War, children, it's just a shot away.
See the fire is sweeping our very street today.
Burns like a red coal carpet.
Mad bull lost its way.
Rape, murder!
The flood is threatening my very life today.
I tell you love, sister, it's just a kiss away.

*

79

You wandered Carlisle's Lakeland International Raceway by yourself that afternoon.

All the teams or gangs or whatever, with their color-coded uniforms, they stood around in the hot dust next to their cars with their flashy paint jobs: yellow and black, red white and blue, white and green.

Every car unfolded on display, hoods flipped open like a long line of pervert flashers.

How boring, you thought.

Did you know what else you would've wanted?

Playing with your hair, you sat in the bleachers alone among the pairs of dudes and couples and dudes alone.

The few women that you did come across all looked at each other like competition for limited resources.

And ever since modeling, you couldn't get the advice of your coach out of your head.

You hated to be outside without sunscreen.

After lining up in oil puddles, red cars raced each other.

One long insect-looking car looked like a dragonfly.

It shot a parachute out behind it to brake.

Cars trailed thick smoke behind them.

You wandered off by the time The 55 came up to the line, but from the parking lot you heard the announcer tinny through the loudspeaker – *Little 55 sounds strong.*

*

James and Dennis had emptied the car to race, and you didn't know where they'd set down your bag.

From afar, he didn't see you, but you watched Warren meander through the lot on his own.

Must've been tired of his own stories.

You moved to approach him, but stopped, figured he must've wanted to be alone or he would've already attached himself to someone.

Strange to watch him across the dusty lot, quiet in the

bright orange and purple of sundown, not quite so desperate on his own, at peace.

You were tired of your own stories.

You must've wanted to be alone or you would've attached yourself to someone.

It was strange to be in the bright orange and purple of sundown without your bag.

*

But by sundown, restless and desperate to get moving again, you fell asleep in the empty backseat of a strange car that you'd never seen before.

You didn't know how long you slept.

The occasional burst of bright beams shocked your vision yellow.

Waking you with a slam of the door, Warren got in the car and sat in the driver's seat.

Your eyes met in the rearview mirror.

I think there's someone following us. – He said, hushed.

You'll get used to it. – You said, playing along cool.

His international-man-of-intrigue-stories could be charming, when they were playful and stripped of the stress of him asking you to actually believe them.

Still you would've appreciated a *real* driver, one of the guys in his real role or being himself: a driver.

A friend of the strange car's owner ducked his head into Warren's open window.

Too drunk or dumb to notice or comprehend that you two didn't belong in the car, he leaned an elbow to the window to detail some plans for after the track: grilling at the lake, skinnydipping in teams.

Going so far as to affect an accent this time, Warren's quick story saved you both for a second time that day.

Still, you had to wonder what it meant that he was willing to just say anything, to lie at any moment.

You had your private island and your pet coyote, sure, but that was the full extent of your own storytelling impulse.

With a spit to the dirt, the yokel shuffled off.

The shared thrill, not laughter but a sustained smiling gaze, having gotten away with something together, joined Warren and you with some new sense of solidarity.

*

While you'd been asleep in the backseat of that strange car, The 55 had returned to the lot and seeing it parked, empty, you returned to it to look for your bag.

While you dug around in the dark backseat, Dennis got in, sat shotgun.

Looking to you in the rear-view mirror, he told you – *we'll be in DC tomorrow after dinner.*

James sat down in the driver's seat.

Strange to each be back in position in the car, but without its growl.

The screech and ripping engines of the track sounded far away.

Looking straight ahead, James announced plainly that he'd set up one last race, the tools against three hundred bucks.

Dennis looked at him then quickly turned away, stifled some response.

James caught your eye.

He didn't smile, didn't seem to attempt to convey any message.

He just looked, a look a little less than his stare.

Stepping out, Dennis finally responded – *I gotta check the valves.*

James turned around in his seat, looked at you.

He cleared his throat and glanced beyond you, cleared his throat again.

With a pleading tone that you'd never heard from him before, like he was bargaining with a pouting child, he said – *After DC we'll go on down to Florida. They got some nice beaches there.*

You didn't respond.

He walked off.

This time you grabbed your bag before they set it aside for the race.

Across the lot, Warren sat in the GTO, his driving gloves already on, hands on the wheel.

*

And soon: the zipping drone of the road, the yellow stripe of the lanes in the beams.

You slept shotgun while Warren drove, but never deeply, your hair in the breeze patting against your face.

He listened to bossa nova.

At some point, after a long while, you became aware that he'd been speaking.

– *And we're just gonna get healthy. Let all the scars heal.*

But you didn't flinch.

And he just kept talking. – *We'll go on. Doesn't matter where.*

When he pulled off at a rest stop, the breaking of momentum startled you.

But you squelched any big moves that might let on that you were awake, rolling over or sitting up.

You just sighed and resettled your weight without cracking open an eye.

You'd learned with plenty of practice that you could get your bearings quick and size up a situation immediately upon waking.

You knew to play possum until that creep made one move.

Sleep was your only potential defense against him making a move out there.

You wondered if James and Dennis had even noticed yet that you'd gone.

You wondered if they would put it together that Warren was gone too.

Maybe they'd catch up.

Warren parked just beyond the glow of the furthest streetlight, closed his eyes and folded his arms, attempting to sleep upright in the driver's seat.

After a few deep breaths he looked over to you with a low groan, hoping to catch your eye.

You didn't need to peek.

That's why he was watching you sleep.

He was waiting to catch you.

You knew how deep the harsh lights would make the folds of his face appear.

His cologne sharp in the still air, you didn't stir.

I'm crazy about you. We'll build a house. – He said.

You didn't even peek.

You didn't let a muscle flutter, not a grind of your jaw would give you away.

You had no problem breathing deep, pretending to sleep through any fear.

You waited out his pause.

Because if I'm not grounded soon – his voice shook – *I'm gonna go into orbit.*

*

You jumped up alert, wide-eyed awake and on defense in no uncertain terms, when Warren touched his leather-gloved hand to your hair and called you – *Baby.*

Parked at a roadside café: early morning, his bossa nova loud without the wind to stifle it, your fuzzy purse in your lap.

You got out of the car, birdsong in the bright air, your neck cramped from sleeping with your head hanging wrong again.

A motorcycle with a bag tied to its back, parked far from the door, over by the parking lot's entrance, was the only other vehicle.

Groggy, you thought, everyone knows about the majesty of birds, the mysterious grace, how they steer as a group.

But traveling, you thought, people travel, submit to the sustained fatigue, only to be able to see the world again, tune into seeing it and overcome the immunities we all build up against our wonder, so we can feel, even if only for a moment, that what we know to be *most* real, the birds for example, their majesty and mystery, these things are in fact real.

Feel real.

Like how you always felt about other people, like they were all more real than you.

The heat hung so solid and still over the dust and sunshine and quiet.

There was nothing else to hear out there but birdsong.

Just your slow shuffle through the lot and into the room.

The screen door creaked, then slammed loud.

*

A young longhaired kid, no older than you, wearing a turtleneck under his denim button-down, sat alone at the counter.

He stared at you when you entered, didn't hide doing so, and turned to continue staring as you crossed the room.

You and Warren sat down at a table, both of your backs turned to the big picture window facing the lot.

You felt stiff in body, stiff in mind and in spirit and mood.

Sleeping sitting up, never really sleeping, afraid to close your eyes entirely on Warren, continuously woozy with half-sleep until driving quiet through the dawn, no longer bothering to pretend to sleep, you must've finally drifted off.

You dreaded sitting down to a meal with him, the beginning of conversation.

Driving, before his first coffee, his bullshit hadn't woken up yet.

Staring straight ahead, sitting side-by-side, keeping quiet came easy.

But at the café, you sat perpendicular.

Groggy, his features already so big on his face, puffed up.

Aching and dazed, communicating nothing more than reciprocity, you returned the kid at the counter's stare.

The waitress approached.

You looked to Warren and he smiled.

His smile widening, his hands extended, he ordered playfully – *Champagne, Caviar.*

You could only sigh.

He ordered eggs over-light and you got only hot tea.

Your stomach was queasy with exhaustion, but also, you sure didn't want to owe Warren anything.

The waitress walked off.

Peripherally, that kid at the counter checked you out and you posed still for him a moment.

Maybe we ought to go to Chicago. – Warren said, sitting up straight. – *I got some connections in Chicago that are out of sight.*

You looked at his face closely, the soft puff of his jowls.

Even kept closely shaven, his skin was rough.

What vanity would compel someone to shave every day in dank gas station men's rooms and rest stops?

His red eyes always looked wet.

I don't want to go to Chicago. – You said.

He shrugged. – *That's cool then. We'll check out New York.*

Warren had said all kinds of things the night before, driving, dark, staring straight ahead, all kinds of things that anyone would've pretended to sleep through to save him the embarrassment.

You know. – He said – *I've been thinking. You keep on the move like this, it catches up with you, you know?*

You never responded, never let on the whole night that you heard a single word of it.

At the café that morning, so quiet, you were afraid, embarrassed to think that he might start that talk again, his voice so loud in the quiet room.

Couldn't you both just pretend none of it had been said?

– I could see myself staying put for a while somewhere. I don't know where, but if you'd come with me we could go wherever you want. The ocean somewhere. Mexico. Hell I've been all over and I know I can do just fine anywhere.

And which was more contrived: his secret C.I.A. missions, his ranch and beach house, his test pilot days, and his stilted swinger-slang – or – his everything-fell-apart-on-me middle-aged desperation to get in your pants?

Together you sat silent.

86

*

You both recognized the growl of the engine pulling up behind you, didn't need to turn and look.

Warren groaned – *Shit.*

You played with your hair, curled it around your finger, pulling your bangs past your nose.

The screen door's stretched springs screeched before it slammed.

You didn't look up at James and Dennis as they entered.

They crossed the restaurant to your table.

You never looked up and didn't think that Warren did, either.

There was a long silence, staring and silent, when they sat down and joined you.

Solemn, Warren nodded hello and got up with a sigh, walked off to the men's room.

He dropped his napkin to the ground as he stood, but quick to step away, he didn't stop to pick it up.

The kid across the café stood up, dropped a couple clanging coins on the counter.

James stared at you.

You looked back at him.

The kid crossed the café, walked over to the coat rack and picked up his jacket.

His hands in his lap, Dennis kept his eyes down.

There was a break, just a slip, a second, but you saw it: a puncture in James's concentrated gaze, his attempt at his hypnosis trick.

Dennis's mouth hung open a little.

James broke the silence, his tone flat, redoubling the mission of his Rasputin stare. – *Figured we'd go up to Columbus, Ohio. There's a man there that's got some parts he wants to sell real cheap.*

You didn't flinch.

You looked back at James, silent.

You could hear Dennis's light panting.

The kid moved to the middle of the restaurant and

stopped, staring at you while he spread his arms wide to put on his coat.

James looked back at you, looked you in the eyes.

You looked James in the eyes.

You didn't sigh.

You didn't tilt your head.

You didn't raise your voice.

You said – *No good.*

Dennis had hairy wrists, thick wrists.

He never looked up from them, his light panting steady.

James's eyes darted around the room then dropped.

He flared his nostrils, inhaled deep and dropped his chin.

Birds chirped.

The screen door slammed closed behind the kid and you were up, pulling on your coat.

None of them said anything.

James glanced up at you.

You walked out the door, its stretching springs creaking, punctuated with a slam.

Across the lot, the kid stood on his motorcycle, turned at the waist, and watching you, knew to wait.

Two young goofs ogled over The 55.

You reached through the open window, grabbed your bag from The GTO.

You crossed the parking lot to the kid, had to throw your big bag off into the bushes before climbing on back, your arms around his waist.

He kickstarted the bike.

With a hard jolt, you were off up the driveway.

*

Out on the bright country road, you smiled and winced against the wind in your face, the speed cooling you in the endless sheets of sunshine.

You felt perfect: no sense of beginning or end, nameless, the constant beat of the wind on your skin a kinetic blur of boundaries.

88

The day was perfect, hot and kept cool moving, nothing to say and no feeling that something should be said.

You felt your lungs inflate with the onrush of scenery and thought "this is what it is to be happy."

You pulled yourself up tight against that kid's back, your hair blowing wildly, without pattern.

*

You rode until just after dusk and sometimes the road would look a little bit familiar to you, like you were circling back where you had come from.

But you could never totally be sure.

All the roads looked the same around that part of the country.

Same as any other part of the country, everywhere looked like itself.

But sometimes you swore you saw specifics: *That* crumbling barn looks like it can't remain balanced, *that* dried-up creek, *that* skeleton of a gas station logo.

But you could never know.

You would've seen everything coming from the other direction before.

And it was dark the last hours you'd been with Warren in the GTO.

Eventually the road lifted a little and straightened and the distance was all blue and rippling, but you knew that it couldn't be water.

I see the earth. It is so beautiful. – The cosmonaut had said.

Was it hills made blue by being seen through clouds?

Was it blue hills in the distance, the hills themselves somehow blue?

The sun moved low enough straight ahead of you, you could make out the lit outlines.

Those blue hills far away were the clouds.

*

You were still looking straight ahead, as always, and still aware not to stop in any one particular place too long.

The motorcycle kid and you checked into a motel.

Stiff weeds curled up from cracked pavement at the door.

You entered the room thick with bleach-smell, the door swollen crooked in its frame.

The motorcycle kid switched on a lamp on the nightstand.

You fell backwards on to the bed and bounced in place a moment, your dusty jeans leaving a pale swatch of dirt on the faded comforter.

The kid walked over to the window and looked back and forth outside quick before pulling the curtain closed.

He returned and sat down next to you.

He was muscular, not bulging but lean, sinewy with perfect baby skin.

His blond hair fell over his brow.

Not quite long enough to stay tucked behind his ear, he brushed it from his eyes constantly.

He looked at you with a purposeful, very serious expression and you sighed before mustering a tired smile.

He touched your hair and you gracefully pulled back a little, smiled again.

He leaned over and kissed you wet and aggressive and you submitted to it.

Pushing his skull hard against yours, his tongue flicking fast.

He ran his palms along the tops of your thighs in a steady rhythm; steady enough that under your jeans your thighs began to burn from friction.

And after a moment, not too soon, but it felt like you'd already waited too long, you put your hands on the back of his to stop his constant motion and break his rhythm.

You retreated from the kiss.

You picked his hands up by the wrists and placed them in his lap.

He grunted – *Ungh*, confused.

You dropped your chin and looked up at him through your

bangs.

You sighed, told him – *I'm gonna take a bath.*

Frustrated, the kid leaned in towards you. – *But I thought* –

Yeah – you cut him off. – *I'll make it with you. It's cool.*

He sat back confident and relieved.

But first I need to take a hot bath. – You said. – *OK?*

Yeah. Sure. – He said. – *OK.*

OK then. – You stood up.

The kid leaned back on the bed on his elbows and tossed his hair as if on display, as if being photographed for a beefcake calendar.

You smiled and leaned over, kissed him on the forehead.

You grabbed your fuzzy purse and carried it along with you.

The thick carpet sticky, you walked into the bathroom and closed the door behind you.

Leaning against the sink, you were free to exhale deep.

*

You ran the bath, curious if those guys had made it to DC.

You pulled off your dusty jeans.

You might've knocked the kid out with the sudden waft released into the air.

You wondered who made it to DC first and won the other's pink slip.

Wiping clean stripes across your face with your finger through caked dust, you looked at yourself in the mirror a good long while.

No shampoo around, but you could at least undo your matted hair with a bar of soap.

No way Warren even had a chance.

The question was whether James and Dennis would actually take his car from him.

Breathing deep, you held your face over the steam of the running bath.

You laid back with your eyes closed, melting into the tub.

*

PART 2

Cockfighter

(1974)

Lying back in the bathtub, half-awake and entirely still, you submitted to hot muscle atrophy.

Drifting among pale color-fields, the pinks and browns of active vision within closed eyes, skating through low clouds, you released your mind from any obligations to its attendant meat.

Then banging on the door jarred you alert, a splash.

And shocked to be thrown back into to your body all at once, you cinched your closed eyes, knowing that some conscious effort to linger wouldn't really make any difference.

Laurie, Sugar – Harry Dean called out in his creaky caterwaul.

You inhaled deep, felt the chill of your chest breaking the surface of the bath water.

Scooting back, you sat up, but didn't respond.

The entirety of your awareness focused on your skin stiffening into goose bumps.

Harry Dean banged again. – *Come on now honey. It's getting to be time, we gotta get on moving.*

Knocking and knocking shamefully loud for the afternoon, it'd be terribly embarrassing if any of the other guests were in their rooms.

They'd think either that you two start drinking that early in the day or you shout at each other like that even when you aren't drinking.

Either way, embarrassing.

Sugar?

And you couldn't take it anymore, but you also didn't know how else to resist.

Ignoring him never worked.

OK – you called out, splashing as you stood, bending at the waist to unplug the drain.

You knew that your voice had moved up in your throat a

little and taken on a bit of a twang, since running around with Harry Dean.

But echoing against the tiles, it surprised you as it still sometimes did when you first spoke out loud after having been quiet awhile.

You'd always had an unconscious bias for self-consciousness.

Maybe that was one more side effect of your mom dying so young, and you quite literally raising yourself.

You tried to shake it, this self-consciousness.

Especially, more and more often, your observations of yourself weren't exactly living up to your ideas of yourself.

You about ready, Sugar?

Yeah, I'm coming.

Well, you know it's getting right on up to five o'clock now and you know the boys are all expecting me.

Must've been in that tub a while.

You didn't know it was so late.

But you said – *I know. I'm coming. I know.*

You grabbed a towel and wrapped it around yourself and stepped out of the tub, and let yourself drip.

Leaning back against the counter, the cool ledge of the sink folded sharply into your ass.

You lit a cigarette, careful not to dampen it between your wet fingers.

Harry Dean knocked. – *Fifteen minutes we gotta be going. I know* – you shouted.

Except for the slow click of the ceiling fan, total quiet followed the punctuating belch of the draining tub.

You heard the scrape of Harry Dean's lean against the door.

His voice lowered, softened. – *I was hoping you might wear that new outfit I bought you, the red one with the hat.*

I will. – You said. – *I got it in here.*

You just look so pretty in that.

I will. – You said again, running your cigarette under the sink.

"The Red One," as if that clarified which outfit.

Just give me a minute. – You said.

*

Lying back on the bed watching television, Harry Dean bent up to a shallow angle when you cracked the bathroom door.

The Rolling Stones' "Wild Horses" was on the small radio.

A good deal older than you, in his mid-forties and tall, Harry Dean wore a white suit with a red and white striped shirt, and a big red ribbon tied around his neck.

You peeked around the door and he sat up towards you.

The light of the television projecting up on him amplified the shadows of his gaunt face.

You shuffled around the door slow, bashful in the red outfit he'd bought you.

He'd been raising the stakes on those outfits and had really outdone himself this time: matching skirt and short coat, matching red-striped knee-high socks and top, and a red hat with a big striped bow that tied it all together.

You felt the outfits were becoming like dares.

Harry Dean picked out all your clothes – always a knee-high something, boots or socks.

He said reds and pinks brought out the subtleties of your complexion against your red hair.

But he never talked about it much, except when you protested.

After looking you over a moment, stunned it seemed, he jumped up at attention and stood straight in front of you and looked you over, feigning he'd lost his breath.

Well honey. – He said in almost a whisper – *You are an angel.*

You smiled. – *You like it?*

He nodded dramatically. – *Oh yes. You look just like an angel, Sugar. You do.*

You could sense yourself blush, embarrassed that you'd let him irritate you as much as you had.

A good, virtuous man, you were lucky that he'd taken you

on and you knew he loved you, the way he doted on you.

And you did like to make him happy.

It made you feel good.

Harry Dean certainly wasn't handsome in the common sense of the word.

But he had a weathered sadness about him, looked sad in a way that even at his happiest it made it hard not to pity him, to like him and to feel for him.

Come on over here and let me get a look at you. – He said.

You took tiny steps on your toes, remaining in place to tease him.

You felt the slight pull in your calves.

He did have a nice profile.

People did sometimes think he was handsome when they'd see him in profile, and then they'd be surprised and let down to see him straight on.

Either way, however handsome or not anyone else ever might've thought he was, that was never what you liked about him.

You might've even thought his modest looks a testament to your own depth of character, your humility.

You were, after all, an ex-model and ever since, you couldn't get the advice of your coach out of your head.

You knew to rub a turnip on your face to blend blemishes.

Come here. – He said again, more commanding, but with a smile.

You approached him slowly.

He took you by one hand and, keeping the same patient pace that you had established with your approach, he lifted your hand over your head and spun you.

Just let me get a look at you.

Completing a full twirl, facing him, he lowered your arm back to your side, and holding your hand firm, he pulled you to him.

My beautiful bride – his voice breathy. – *You have made me the proudest man in The Southern Conference, you have.*

He bumped his nose to yours lightly and widened his eyes.
– *Hell, the proudest man in The South.*

You squirmed.

He said – *I love you* and you nodded and said you loved him too.

He tilted your head to his chest, but the folds of your hat and that big bow pinned to it kept your head leaning awkwardly.

I am going to take care of you and you will never have nothing to worry about ever again. You hear me?

You nodded and smiled.

Alright now, Sugar. – He said, patting you on the shoulder and standing up straight. – *Now let's get on over there and make me some money, OK?*

You told him that you'd be up there in the stands, watching, taking photos.

I know you will honey.

You told him – *I'll be cheering for you, so you just look out for me.*

I will be honey. – He said. – *I will.*

*

Loud with the crowd's cheers and chatter, the birds' flutters and squawks and screams, the barn was wide and long and tall, dusty enough to tickle the back of your throat.

The air dry and still, aluminum walls held in the heat.

The bleachers, filled to capacity, always all men, hollering, surrounded the ring set up in the center.

A few glaring floodlights reflecting on the dirt lit the ring, which had been drawn out in chalk and bordered by small walls halfway up to one's knee.

Barbed wire shimmered.

Looking around, you thought this crowd would probably smell the same even gathered together in a sparkling clean ballroom without any birds around killing each other, without the stench of death.

The men in suits and the men in overalls traveled to every tournament.

One bloated-Elvis in an unbuttoned pajama top, irate,

waved and pointed at the chalkboard.

A young kid, trying to be hip with a headband, watched the fight closely.

Aware that hipness was even a thing, like some materialized echo from your past life, you wondered how did that kid end up there?

You tried not to pose for him.

You couldn't even know for sure if he even noticed you, but he had to.

The way Harry Dean dressed you up as his warped ideal of domesticated rag-doll, you were still modeling.

He dressed you up as if to squash or conceal any possibility of someone realizing how sexy you just were on your own, unaffected.

And realizing that you were still somebody's model was the only thing in the world that ever could've made you miss modeling.

*

Off in a corner beyond the ring, Harry Dean gave Warren a cigarette and lit it for him before lighting his own.

Warren was Harry Dean's fiercest rival, the only man that posed any sort of threat to his title.

The men in the conference all thought of Warren as one ruthless motherfucker.

He supposedly once even sold a house out from under his own brother, to afford a new truck and birds.

This cutthroat reputation was quite a difference from both the sad-sack stories of everything falling apart on him, and the outlandish tales of espionage that he used to tell when you first met him.

But however he may have changed, he was still pathetic to you.

You watched the two men contentedly watch the match together, Harry Dean in his Candy Land suit and Warren in all-denim.

Warren hadn't spoken even one word in the last couple

years, not a peep.

But when you were with him, when you two were a couple before Harry Dean and you got together, Warren did talk in his sleep.

Back in those days, racing his GTO when you first met, you would've sworn there was nothing you'd have wished for more than Warren to be struck mute.

But his pig-headed charade of being struck mute was just a whole new way he'd found to irritate people.

*

Harry Dean leaned in close, talking into Warren's ear.

Leaning back on his heels, Warren nodded one quick, authoritative nod.

From across the barn, the body language of their conversation looked funny: one moving his mouth, yammering, pausing only for the other to nod that he'd heard him.

Harry Dean flashed an open palm: five fingers spread, then held up two fingers.

They shook hands curtly.

You never did understand the point systems and odds and all that of cockfighting.

Seemed simple enough to you: my bird attacks your bird and your bird attacks mine, and we'll see which bird lives.

But it did get complex, scoring and point-spreads and such.

Throwing his shoulders back, his chest puffed out with effort, Harry Dean put his hands to his hips and looked over the room, his gaze drifting, not really aiming to take any detail in.

Warren watched him do this.

You were embarrassed for Harry Dean and his struggle to be himself.

Harry Dean turned to Warren and Warren looked away.

*

When he sighed deeply and kicked a toe to the dirt, you knew that Harry Dean must've been starting the talk that he told you he'd have with Warren.

You were embarrassed for yourself for being with Harry Dean.

This talk that he'd been planning was as memorized as Warren's old speech about his GTO once was – *Hard pull, zero to sixty in seven-point-five.*

You were certain Harry Dean would begin, as you'd heard him say quite some many times by then – *So don't suppose you've heard the good news?*

Warren looked up at him sideways and shrugged, shook his head.

Harry Dean, eyes lowered, spoke.

Warren raised his eyebrows and held them raised.

Harry Dean must've told him he'd gotten hitched.

From across the barn, you could practically read Harry Dean's lips, knowing his spiel and the timing of his mannerisms.

Yes sir. I did boy. I know, I never thought I would again either, you know. What with this life we live, on the road, the motels, and the drinking and the hot heads – the stink of The Sport. But uh, she's really something you know. She just took me. I was taken by her. Yeah boy, I was.

Surveying the bleachers, Harry Dean caught your eye, caught you watching them.

He blew you a kiss.

You smiled and waved back.

Warren nodded, tipped his hat to you.

You looked away quickly, pretending to be absorbed in some development in the ring.

You hoped that the talk would go exactly as Harry Dean told you it would, as he had practiced it, the whole time telling you he wasn't nervous, even as his phrasings solidified through repetition.

She says you can talk – Harry Dean would say and Warren would be taken aback.

Now no need to be nervous. Of course I know all about

you two, and I don't mind one bit, because you know? Who are you gonna tell, right?

Harry Dean chuckled and Warren grinned and nodded.

Yep, he must've paced the joke precisely as he'd planned it.

But she says you talk in your sleep. Says you're angry too.

Warren shook his head.

Yeah, I know, I know it's crazy. But she's just got it in her head that you can talk. And she's afraid you might say something about you and her.

Warren drooped his shoulders and looking Harry Dean squarely in the eyes, his expression demonstratively sincere, shook his head, no.

I mean you know how women are.

Warren nodded solemnly.

You know, she wanted me to talk to you. Make sure. That's all.

Warren looked him in the eye and offered his hand.

Harry Dean smiled and shook his hand slow, holding it a moment.

Well, thank you. Thanks. She'll just feel better if I can tell her I talked to you.

Warren nodded.

Harry Dean slapped him on the shoulder and turned to shuffle off.

Alright. Alright. I'll see you in the ring.

Warren smiled his big toothy grin.

He looked back up at you in the bleachers, and you dropped your camera quickly.

*

Warren drank too much and talked too much.

Back when he cruised the country in his GTO, he had that speech about his car down verbatim for all the hitchhikers he'd pick up.

Hard pull, zero to sixty in seven-point-five.

But the lies were all improvised, changing each trip.

He repeated the same stories with his details jumping

103

wildly one telling to the next: this time a test pilot, this time a Top Secret mission.

After he'd had enough of crisscrossing the country, cockfighting drew him in: some new subculture to attach himself to, find himself in.

And he was good – one of the best.

But eventually, shooting his mouth off cost him the Southern Conference title.

Harry Dean took great pleasure in retelling you the story of that night Warren blew the title, the tragedy and hard lessons learned.

Every couple weeks, every time any of the younger fighters prodded Harry Dean into socializing, especially after a big win, it was Harry Dean's prize, submitting to his compulsion to tell that story one more time, every time as if he had never told anyone before.

Drunk on the eve of the championship, Warren kept swinging a chicken around a hotel room, bragging, and Harry Dean finally challenged him to a battle at 2 AM, just to shut him up.

Warren lost the chicken that would've won him the championship.

He had to withdraw.

And after the death of that chicken that night in that motel room, he never spoke again.

But he didn't fool you.

If he could talk in his sleep, then he could talk when he was awake.

You understood what it was.

You understood Warren.

He'd learned to fly a plane and lost interest in it.

Water skiing, and lost interest in it.

But cockfighting was something you didn't conquer.

He really was that proud, that dedicated to conquering something, being a master of something.

And even when a person is as self-absorbed and fixated on one thing, as Warren was with game fowl, even if that person can't talk – or won't, for whatever reason – you still live with someone in a small trailer and you pick up little bits of things.

You learned more about him living with him as a mute than you ever did when he was a babbling compulsive liar.

*

Warren came from Mansfield, Georgia, a small town with no curbs, and train tracks cutting through it.

His brother needed a shot of whiskey with his morning coffee to steady his hand.

He and his wife lived in Warren's house.

Every six months or so, Warren would circle back to get money from them.

Every time they wondered if that time he might not stay.

He had a true love back there, who would tell rambling stories with abstract moral lessons while he undid her blouse.

*

That night Warren got struck silent in the motel room – that night before the championship, that was right before you and Warren found each other again.

You hardly recognized him when you met again and he was silent.

It had been a couple, three years.

But you fell right back in with each other.

Real soon after the reunion, he once even pointed at you when someone asked him about family.

Maybe the attraction for you was just the obvious change that he'd been through.

Maybe he was just so much *more* attractive, having finally shut up, that you mistook that for attractive at all, not just contextually– or relatively– attractive.

But it did make you reconsider your entire past.

You remembered everything differently, him and how you were together.

And it was thanks to Warren that you eventually ended up

Mrs. Harry Dean Stanton.

*

Coming up against each other cockfighting, that wasn't the first time Warren and Harry Dean had met.

Warren knew it, but he never did know if Harry Dean didn't remember him or if he just didn't acknowledge it because frankly, if it was true how Warren insisted it happened – and he'd become a pretty reliable truth-teller ever since he stopped talking – you wouldn't be surprised if Harry Dean didn't enjoy ruminating on it.

But same as Harry Dean enjoyed telling the story of Warren's big loss, Warren used to like to tell the story – in his way, of course, miming and answering yes-or-no questions – of the night he and Harry Dean had first met.

It was that same race across America that he and you first met, the marathon, that he first met Harry Dean.

Warren picked up Harry Dean alongside the road in a straw cowboy hat and denim suit, heading to Oklahoma City.

Warren insisted that he'd never forgotten a face, all the hitchhikers he'd picked up.

Harry Dean, when he stretched out shotgun saying that he was going to try to get some shut-eye, tilting the tip of his hat down on his nose, he reached over and put his hand on Warren's knee.

Warren gave him a stern warning.

And when he did it again some hours later, after getting through a tense quiet and back to friendly chitchat, Warren pulled over to kick him out into the rain in the middle of the night in the middle of nowhere.

Harry Dean sniffled and pouted, refusing to leave.

Warren was so embarrassed for him that he agreed to bring Harry Dean as far as the next town before kicking him out.

Years later, losing the title in some lousy motel room at 2 AM to a man that he'd met in that way, such a loss struck Warren mute.

The chickens hopping over each other's backs, it always seemed like slow motion, a dream-image the way the torn feathers floated, making everything else appear accelerated by contrast.

Kicks to the neck, biting each other's throats out, biting down on the other's beak, bite down on the back of the neck, a kick to the head.

And by the end, only a couple minutes later, Warren would be done talking.

And of course you never asked Harry Dean to confirm or deny that story of how Warren insisted that the two of them had first met.

*

When you were with Warren, he was totally indifferent about you watching his matches or not.

Free to wander in or out as you chose to, you enjoyed the matches you did watch.

But things weren't like that with Harry Dean, always needing to look up and see you in the stands in whatever knee-high and bubblegum pink getup he'd insisted on that day.

What a curse to have him so convinced that you brought him luck: you, in red or pink specifically.

Warren's bigheadedness: at least it wasn't dandy vanity.

You never slept with Warren before his vow of silence, but you always imagined that he really must've become a much better lay after he shut up.

Shutting up, he started channeling all his energy differently.

He lost the ascot.

And maybe he listened in a way that he never could before.

Hearing people for the first time after a lifetime of babbling, maybe that made him aware of other people's feelings.

He had those strong hands.

The thought of you with anyone else ...

And he was a brute, but he fucked like his brutishness was

all for your sake.

You couldn't imagine that that would've been the case back when all he did was talk and talk to try to impress everyone.

Harry Dean's soft touch, its tenderness might've seemed to be more for your sake, deferential and more considerate than brutishness would be, but really it was all about the satisfaction that he got from touching you softly.

Shutting up freed Warren, allowed him to inhabit the world differently, changed the terms of every negotiation.

Even with bare feet, he might jump off a porch with sudden joy or climb over the top of a car on his belly like a spider.

Harry Dean couldn't do that.

His decorum would never allow it.

But they were both still cockfighters, so certain offenses to your sensibilities were a given.

Any good cockfighter occasionally had to duck back into his corner and put a bird's head in his mouth to calm it down when it got too excited.

Thinking of this, you squirmed, held back, pulled away, any time either of them ever leaned in to kiss you.

*

Harry Dean, not even bashful asking you, always wanted you to take his picture out there in the ring.

You'd first picked up an old camera when living with Warren.

Happy as you may have been together, those could get to be some pretty boring times for you, traveling around with him while he was still figuring out to what degree and by what means he'd communicate.

The days were one long evolving game that blended Charades and Twenty Questions.

You often had to remind him that even if you did accept that he really couldn't speak, you knew that he could still hear you.

So you took up taking pictures.

You liked the mechanical old camera, levers and bolts and

108

fabric folded into accordions, unsure exactly how to hold it without it pinching your fingers.

And then the images: Warren removed from time, a time before, a time which, when passing as any time did, kinetic, you never really did get a good-enough look at.

You snapped away and then weeks would pass.

When you got near enough to a town and would be staying for a couple days, you'd drop off all the film.

By the time you could look back over what you'd shot, little of it would even look familiar.

Warren complained if he thought that you pointed the camera at him too much.

But still he'd give you money to get the film developed and buy new film.

He pretended to be uninterested when you'd return to the park after a long walk into town to pick up the photos.

You'd spread them all out on a picnic table so you could see all of them at once, line them up in order to tell the story of your previous weeks.

You would pick up one at a time, hold it close to your nose and study it, study all you had missed as you lived through it.

Just familiar things; you didn't seek out adventures.

But you did learn how to focus on the background.

Warren would study the photos along with you, many of them of him.

He was always awfully curious about those photos of himself, imagining how he thought he must appear to others.

When he figured out what you were doing in a particular photo – he was in focus, but not in the foreground – he smiled and nodded at you, proud.

He figured out what you had been fooling around with, this selective focus: a technique that as far as you knew, you might've invented yourself.

Seeing that photo of himself in focus in the background, he understood all the photos that he'd previously flipped through and thought were just an amateur's failures.

He had to look back over all of those, reconsider them.

*

Warren and Harry Dean each stood in a corner of the ring, feet planted, holding a bird to his chest.

They called this "billing" their birds: swinging them towards each other to get them riled up to fight.

Upon release, either out of true antagonism or just the thrilled confusion of the volume, the vexed birds lunged, pecking at each other.

The audience cheered.

Harry Dean and Warren both pressed back to the sides of the ring to stay out of the way.

In between rounds, each man patted his bird down to keep it alert, give it a jolt.

Squatting down low to give his dazed bird a pep talk, Harry Dean in his saddle shoes tripped and fell sideways.

You snorted a little chuckle, a honk.

Maybe he'd gotten tangled up in his loosely looped tie hanging halfway to his waist, you thought.

But recovering his balance, his fingertips to the dirt, he looked up directly at you in the stands and you immediately regained your composure.

You cleared your throat, straightened your floppy red hat.

You couldn't help but want to cheer for the red bird, but you weren't sure; that might've been Warren's chicken.

*

The second round ended immediately.

The way those birds tangled up in each other in battle, they often had to be unraveled before anyone could even tell whose bird had been killed.

Warren's bird's gaffs, the spikes tied to each chicken at the ankles, poked through the loosely hanging neck of Harry Dean's bird.

The audience whooped.

There was one other woman there.

You hadn't noticed her before, because she blended in easily with all the men.

Harry Dean and Warren, good sports, shook hands.

With a wave over his shoulder to the crowd, Harry Dean exited the ring with the dead bird hanging in his grip.

His shoulders thrown back, nose tilted at a regal incline, Warren moved to the center of the ring and posed with a hotshot sneer.

You could just hear him saying – *Hard pull, zero to sixty in seven-point-five.*

He may have had everyone else convinced that he'd gone mute, but pulling his pants up by the belt buckle, a proud wiggle of the shoulder as he spun to gloat: he was still the same Warren that you had always known.

Arrogant and vain, performative gruff.

Same Warren he had always been. – *Are we still racing or what? I've got speed to think about.*

And he just kept standing there, turning in the center of the ring, that sneering smile of his, basking in his victory.

Was he hearing trumpets in his head?

Did he expect a pyramid built in his honor?

If he'd only walked off like everyone else did, if he hadn't stood around gloating, it wouldn't have happened.

But he didn't, so it did happen.

Your irritation with him just kept building.

He stood there that long that – yes, you had enough time to consider your own irritation and that it was not abating and eventually, after, Jesus Christ, he'd been standing up there posturing with his goddamn big toothy smile quite long enough the conceited son of a bitch and finally – you could just no longer control yourself.

While he waved to the stands opposite you, you charged the ring and hit him hard over the back of his head with your purse.

With surprise to your advantage, you got a good first wallop in.

But returning to swing at him again, he spun you and used the momentum of your own lunge against you, knocking you to the ground.

Smiling that big toothy grin, holding you back, he laughed

at you to the audience, making you into some kind of spontaneous rodeo clown.

And that only made your rage swell more.

You swung and flailed at him.

You aimed to scratch his eyes out, tear that goddamn toothy smile from his big, ugly face.

Swinging continuously, you fell to the dust again and popped right back up.

So wild, your balance all thrown off, Harry Dean came running back into the ring, grabbed you from behind, and threw you over his shoulder easily.

He turned to step away, but with a grin, Warren stopped him and handed him your purse.

Even thrown over Harry Dean's shoulder, the wind knocked from your gut, you kept swinging at Warren during the handoff.

And you saw it.

It was just a second between the men, a glance into each other's eyes held just an extra half-second.

But they said everything they had to say to each other with a sigh and a shrug.

They'd come to some understanding between them.

Warren grinned and Harry Dean shook his head.

Of course the crowd's applause grew louder than ever.

One bearded man in overalls, you had seen him around a lot with Warren those days, turned to another man in the stands as you were carried past him.

What do you think the odds were on Mrs. Stanton? – He joked.

And from the barn door, you saw Warren in the hanging dust your scuffle had thrown up, silhouetted in the ring.

Swinging his hat over his head, he conducted the cheers.

*

You did kiss Warren on the mouth once back then, riding with Dennis and James in the marathon.

It was less than a make out, but more than a peck.

You weren't expecting it to happen and then it happened.

And you never expected it to happen again.

The rain had died down for a while in the middle of the night.

Warren was ahead of you guys and got pulled over.

Coming up on him at the side of the road with some small town cop, James stopped.

He got out and approached the cop, told them that this guy Warren was dangerous, weaving all over the road and passing on the right.

He even offered to be a witness, before peeling out in front of the cop and disappearing into the darkness.

Entering Oklahoma, just leaving Texas, Warren caught back up, honking and wanted to talk.

With only a couple silos lit in the distance visible beyond the cars' beams, you pulled over to have a laugh.

Warren was livid.

Until James blew it for him, he'd talked the cops into giving him a police escort to the state line, believing that his wife was in labor with twins.

Dennis offered him a hard-boiled egg.

Warren opened his trunk, had a fancy wet bar in it.

Poured each of you a Scotch.

He toasted James – *To your destruction.*

And smiling, James responded – *And to yours.*

It was funny how Warren drove Harry Dean so nuts sometimes by refusing to match his level of agitation, keeping his cool when Harry Dean tried to provoke him.

James had taught Warren this skill against his rivals, and you'd witnessed it.

Took years of practice, even took going so far as a vow of silence, but eventually Warren would become the one to keep his cool.

You and Warren sat together in the GTO while Dennis poked around under its hood by the light of The 55's headlights.

Warren talked.

Through the windshield you watched James and Dennis

and couldn't hear them, but they mimicked driving, sudden pulls at the wheel and gearshifts with big gestures.

Warren said – *Listen, why don't you ride with me? We could go to Miami, Montreal, Mexico. Just keep moving.*

You thought of the mimes playing tennis in *Blowup*.

You told Warren you didn't know, not right then.

You told him he'd probably lose the race anyways.

Stunned with pain, he appeared to you at that moment stripped of his daredevil playboy costume, as no more or less than any other old man living with disappointment, collar turned up against the cold, content throwing seeds to feed the pigeons.

He insisted – *I'm serious you know? I'm not just kidding around.*

And that's when you kissed him.

It was more than you would kiss a hurt child, but less than you would kiss a lover.

Dennis told him that he needed to stop for some repair, the GTO wouldn't hold out.

Told him you'd all wait with him in the next town while he got it.

*

That's when you ended up stopping in Boswell.

Dennis drove the GTO to give Warren a break and a chance to ride in The 55.

James rolled his eyes when Warren, climbing in The 55, said – *Not too comfortable in here.*

Riding with Dennis, you sang a continuous associative-medley, picking up a song in its middle straight out of the middle of another, relaxed and excited to know that you'd be pulling off somewhere to sleep a few hours, some small town, a moment to puncture the marathon drift.

Dennis smiled at you, even his eyes happy, every time your song leapt to a parallel track.

When James pulled up alongside you two, the guys' true motive became apparent.

114

They wanted to test the GTO, see how fast it could be pushed.

You and Dennis laughed wildly at Warren sitting shotgun in The 55 at full-throttle, the unguarded shock on his face, his mind obviously blown.

He had to get it then.

He had no chance against The 55.

That next morning, after you'd walked off into the fields and James came and found you and he was going to teach you to drive but you couldn't get it, then James told you that during that test-drive, after slowing down, the research completed and point proven, Warren started to tell him – *Everything fell apart on me: my job, my family.*

But James told him that he couldn't hear about it.

It wasn't his problem.

And then you and James laughed at Warren for that.

James had just found you in those fields the color of singed cheese.

You had to head back to that gas station to pick up Dennis and Warren.

And Warren was somehow then so unlikable that you two laughed at him for trying to tell the truth for once – *Everything fell apart on me: my job, my family.*

In the shade of the short buildings back closer to town, the ground was still damp.

You had just made it with James, parked out in the singed cheese.

But licking at your lips, you could smell it on your own breath, the Scotch and hard-boiled egg from Warren's kiss the night before.

Warren didn't get silence at all until he did.

*

Out on the road after losing the match, Harry Dean pushed the station wagon harder than he usually did when pulling the trailer, especially on those back-roads with their sudden bumps and twists.

The chickens must have been getting thrown all over back

there.

You leaned against the passenger side window, looked up at the trees passing overhead.

At least you no longer had to wonder who you might have to make it with just to get by.

But you still didn't like having to wonder every night whether old Harry Dean would climb on you or not.

Irate, he lectured you.

– *Cockfighting, my dear, may be the only fair contest left in America. No god damned pit chicken could throw a fight if you wanted him to. For you to act out like that humiliates not only you, but it makes a fool of me. I have devoted my life to The Sport, and I have come to be known and trusted within the circuit as a man of integrity and honor.*

The station wagon was grinding.

You watched the flickering of trees passing overhead.

*

Always with a considered opinion and an open ear, Monte reminded you of how you wished that your dad or your brother might've been.

Maybe that's how Harry Dean first appeared to you too.

But Monte really did seem to not want anything from you.

You were still with Warren when Monte asked you about your interest in photography.

He asked if you wouldn't mind just sort of always taking pictures, for the sake of the greater community.

Monte was the head of the whole thing, the organizer of The Southern Conference.

You didn't particularly like the idea of being accountable to anyone else, being required to take a certain number of pictures or pictures of certain things.

But Monte explained that it was exactly the candid moments of living within The Southern Conference that he wanted.

Said you were free to shoot whatever you saw as you saw it.

And that he wanted nothing more than for you to continue

doing exactly what you'd already been doing.

And you knew Warren would appreciate your hobby getting financed.

So you agreed.

Not in any quantifiable way, but your habit of always having a camera slung over your shoulder became a bit more demonstrative: no longer covert, now endorsed and justified.

Monte even gave you a modern camera.

He said that he didn't want fooling around with that antique technology to get in the way of you shooting what you saw.

Handing you the gift, you got embarrassed when in passing he complimented your knee-high socks.

These knee-high socks Warren insisted that you wear were the only continuity between how he and Harry Dean both insisted on dressing you up.

*

Those state park afternoons, colorful torn feathers floated like the flicker of a flame in slow motion, some autumnal snowfall.

Sometimes you sat in the back seat of the station wagon and massaged Harry Dean's shoulders while he drove and talked.

A gamecock bred from a father and a daughter is gonna run every time, you see? No two ways about it. But, a mother and a son, well, you match them up and you got yourself a cock with the biggest heart for fighting to the death that you're ever going to see. But breeding is only part of it. You need know-how in conditioning and a good country walk.

You'd get to the room.

You'd head straight for the bath.

The tubs were often mucky in those cheap motels, so you'd give it a quick superficial rinse with your open palm, using whatever shampoo was around.

Then you'd lay there with your head thrown back and your ears just below the surface of the water.

Had to drown out the sound of the television and Harry Dean, laughing by himself in the next room if he'd won that day, kicking walls and cursing everything if he had lost.

*

You always remembered that line from *The Bell Jar* because you read when it came out when you were living in New York and it felt so true.

"I am sure there are things that can't be cured by a good bath but I can't think of one."

Back in New York, modeling when you were sixteen, that was when the baths first became your sanctuary.

You had your friend the other model to thank for that.

She often talked on the phone without consideration that some details, even one side of a conversation, might occasionally best be left vague for the benefit of third parties.

Coming home to your shared studio apartment and finding her on the phone, heading straight to the bath became a habit, and then a compulsion.

You listened to the radio to block out her chatter and the click of her gum like she was tapping on a woodblock.

Seemed like a long time ago.

And four years was plenty of time for everything to change.

Back then, a teenage model in Manhattan, you certainly never pictured yourself married to Harry Dean – a man in his *forties*, living on the road.

Cockfighting.

You never imagined you might someday miss modeling, a means to an end.

*

Rainy days, of course people internalized.

Manhattan streets, both shining and muted, every orange, brown and green unified through infinite grays.

Drenched, you sat on the bed and peeled off your jeans, your damp thighs sticking a little to the fuzzy blanket.

118

You stood and finished undressing.

You walked into the bathroom.

Sitting on its lip, watching the tub as it filled, you listened to the newscast.

Short months after the Kent State shootings, officials have determined that of the nine students wounded by the National Guard, none were closer than seventy-one feet from the guardsmen and of the four students killed, the nearest was 265 feet away. Critics of the National Guard point to this as evidence that the guardsmen's claims of self-defense are hollow, and they are calling for renewed protests.

Injustice once surprised you, made you outraged only the year before, when you first began to follow and understand the news.

Slowly, slowly you lowered your feet to touch the water's hot surface.

In no hurry to submerge them, you raised your feet slowly as the surface rose.

The announcement came today that the first tenants of the World Trade Center are now just months away from moving in. Construction of David Rockefeller's urban renewal project to revitalize Lower Manhattan has been speed along by the extensive use of prefabricated components –

You spun and leaned to turn off the radio.

Only after the bottom of your feet had acclimated to the heat of the water did you finally break the surface, and plunge your feet under up to your ankles.

You took a long time to get in that tub, longer than any other bath in your life had taken you.

Swirling steam assisted you in discerning melodies hidden in the faucet's roar.

In the back of your mind, ever since, you've always wanted to come home with that same degree of chill, that same ratio of feeling internalized on busy downtown streets.

Bathwater could be standardized, and lighting kind of.

*

You had seen Harry Dean around a couple times, milling about with a paper plate piled high at a picnic table.

Maybe a polite hello over the coleslaw and potato salad.

He always wore his ties in long, loose bows dangling halfway down his chest.

He never wore a hat and along with that long chin of his, and his sad eyes, it was hard not to notice him.

But you never paid him much mind.

Until later, when you blamed him and thought him a scoundrel.

You shouted at him. – *I never heard of someone taking away someone's home before.*

And Warren walking off, silent of course, across the gravel of the RV lot in the heat, silent and smug even after losing his car, his trailer and you, his girl, all in one chicken battle.

You shouted at him. – *What about me?*

Children paused in the woodchips near the garbage cans, looked at you.

Harry Dean stared at the toes of his white boots.

Holding his breath, he seemed to be stuck in the middle of a sigh.

I don't need you. – You called out after Warren.

And he kept walking, walking away.

You called after him. – *Take me with you. I don't want to stay with old Harry Dean.*

Warren didn't even look back.

But you knew him.

You knew the subtleties of his sense of his emotional obligations, his finely tuned justifications.

You were certain he distinguished: he felt *sorry* for you, but wasn't *afraid* for you.

To you at that moment, that distinction made no difference and meant nothing.

*

You always thought something changed in Warren after

that race against Dennis and James, the marathon.

Sure, you didn't know him before that, but you did know how he was when you three met him.

That man you met wasn't about to take on a vow of silence.

And by the time you split from those guys, he'd already started to pick up James and Dennis's story as his own.

All the storytelling he did, that sponge, he picked it up from paperbacks and spy movies and everyone he met, like some kind of precocious child.

But picking up James and Dennis's story as his own, he understood their satisfaction: building something with their own hands, something that could beat his own Detroit-made hot rod.

He understood that he himself had somehow ended up the bad guy in that scenario.

And he struggled for a long time to articulate it, the perspective of the bad guy.

But eventually, he sure did learn to embody it OK.

*

And eventually he came to understand that position well enough, Warren could walk off, rolling a cigarette as he walked, his hat pulled down low over his eyes.

His silence, his cool march, his sense of stoic virtue could say a lot.

That fight – the fight that Warren lost you and his truck and his trailer – Harry Dean had a handler in the ring working his bird for him.

Harry Dean even wore a white suit into the ring.

Maybe he was standing back while the handler got up in there, but a white suit in the ring?

You had never seen that.

If he didn't really have a bigger operation in the past, he at least sure liked to present himself as some kind of aristocrat in exile.

*

You'd been riding along with Warren for a while.

He'd drive with his hand on your knee while you scanned the dial, never anything on the radio on those backroads through the southeast.

Warren thought the trailer was tidy if he kept a sheet thrown over the chicken cages, the cages stacked among the sparse furniture.

Try to sleep through that cock-uh-doodle-doo cacophony come dawn.

You wore your hair in long braids, like you maybe would've when you were a little girl.

You wore tiny T-shirts and short shorts and knee-high socks and Warren loved dressing you up like a little kid, the pervert.

You'd wash his clothes in a big spaghetti pot on the stove.

It was a good enough life that, stupidly, and probably for the first time ever, you weren't looking towards the end of, thinking about the next thing.

Every day was different enough *and* you could settle into a routine.

Then Harry Dean put up $900 against Warren's car and the trailer and you.

At the Weigh-In, Warren cut some feathers off quickly so the bird would make weight.

The fighters knew it made no difference, but the folks placing bets needed to get a sense the match was even.

That was obvious to you even before Warren explained it.

Whoever called the coin-toss got to decide short gaffs or long.

No time limit, no draw, the audience shouting, all of them with their mouths full of chewing tobacco and tobacco spit.

The birds lunged and snapped at each other, their feathers spiking up on their backs like hissing cats.

Over and over, they hopped over each other.

The bleachers were down wind from the dumpster of dead birds.

Tiny watermelon-seed-sized bugs swarmed above it in the stench.

And that was it.

Striking his bird's bill as Warren did to swell the bets wasn't illegal, but you knew he wasn't proud of it.

Might've helped him make some money on the back end, but it did nothing to secure you or his truck and trailer.

Pulling away, everyone else all said goodbyes to each other for a few days until the next tournament – *have a good drive*, or whatever.

Harry Dean welcomed you into his life: surprised it seemed, to find that you came with the trailer.

He comforted you about Warren handing you off to him.

And that was the first intimacy of any kind between you two.

And you appreciated it, didn't think to question it.

*

Eventually, Harry Dean didn't like you going around anywhere without your camera, and he didn't like you pointing your camera at anything but him.

You knew to always shoot him from at least a little bit of an angle.

He never said it, but he knew as well as everyone else did that he didn't look as good straight on.

Sometimes after a victory, he'd run up, panting, his eyes dilated and wide.

He'd ask excitedly if you'd gotten a picture of a particular moment.

He would be so disappointed if you hadn't.

Mostly, the fights all looked all the same to you, the whole time, one moment to the next.

So you learned to just say yes, you had shot everything; hope that by the time the photos came back without some specific moment, he would've forgotten which moment it was exactly that he wanted.

He'd flip quick past any photos he wasn't in, glance at you irritated.

Lingering a moment longer over any photo of himself

straight on, he had to cope with and make sense of seeing himself not from that most flattering three-quarters angle.

*

The one big point of disagreement with Harry Dean that you learned to just keep quiet about, even if every day it was on your mind, was birth control.

The consistency of traveling with him did come with a lot of little perks: the opportunity and the funds to keep tampons and razors on hand, and makeup.

But you had to live with the constant tension of wishing for your period.

You never forgot to count the days.

And still every month there were a couple days of dread, the fear of being late.

And then there was the occasional other wives and girlfriends.

They were sparse and appeared inconsistently.

But you were expected to interact with them as equals, even if they would just mimic their husbands dutifully.

You thought that made them even worse than the men.

One afternoon, loading up at the pharmacy, you picked up a fashion magazine.

Your friend the other model was there in a spread, designer jeans.

She looked the same, maybe better than before with her hair slightly asymmetrical.

Her makeup was under control.

You thought that maybe you'd like to somehow find your old friend Dee Dee from high school.

But how would you ever find her?

And if you did, how could you ever admit to her where you were?

*

You were sprawled out on your belly in bed, the cool top-sheet tangled between your legs.

The light in the window dim behind him, Harry Dean dressed slowly, always.

That man luxuriated in the process of dressing.

He shook you lightly. – *Five AM already, sweetheart.*

You moaned and rolled over.

He sat down, crowding you on the bed and shook you again. – *Come on now. Get a move on.*

He stood up, walked into the bathroom.

With a deep sigh, you sat up with great effort, your own weight more than you could ever imagine lifting from that mattress.

*

You sat shotgun with your eyes closed, and he just kept talking.

So I don't know. Prometheus is good. He's gonna be a four-fight winner by the end of next month, no doubt. And I've never heard of another Prometheus. And why it's such a fitting name for this chicken, all I can figure is no one ever had the nerve to name a chicken Prometheus before. But I think he's gonna live up to it. I do.

Whenever he got quiet for a second, you knew to expect a tap on the knee.

You opened your eyes and he was looking at you, just waiting.

You turned to him and smiled, tired, and he started up again.

Now, Perseus is a fine name. Don't get me wrong. But I think it's gonna have to be Prometheus. I'm ready for it. This is the bird.

You turned back to look out the window.

*

Applying your makeup in the scratched-up and warped metal mirror of a state-park ladies room, one afternoon, you gave up and left your lipstick and rouge smeared in wide swoops.

Your reflection was a blur.

Harry Dean had sent you to the ladies room, insisting that you shave your legs.

Turning to walk out, the cheers of a cockfight in the distance, you paused at the sink.

You took a pull from the small bottle of vodka in your purse to steady yourself before walking out, big stupid red bow stuck at a tilt on your big stupid hat, striped to match your thigh-highs.

*

First time you met Warren, you never ever would've believed it if someone told you that you would someday miss that guy.

Through two or three states, he'd occasionally pass The 55, honking and waving, always with a different hitchhiker shotgun.

It happened right after you'd jumped in with James and Dennis and they explained that it'd happened before.

After Santa Fe you stopped for gas at the far side of the desert, and within a cluster of trailers and churches, big propane tanks and no other cars, there stood Warren, ascot neat and loose around his neck, leather driving-gloves in hand, with his ostentatious yellow GTO.

You walked in on his hitchhiker, a nerd in a cowboy-suit, sitting on the toilet in the ladies room.

He came out so embarrassed that he grabbed his bag and ran across the street to wait for another ride.

Too absorbed in staring down James, Warren didn't even notice the hitchhiker split.

He set his half-drank bottle of Coke back down on the rack with the new bottles – picked it up again, put it down again.

He wanted you three to see him.

For a few long minutes even after the GTO had been filled up and looked over, he waited around doing nothing.

Finally he approached James, his voice like some rupture he had struggled to suppress.

– *I don't like being crowded by a couple of punk road-hogs clear across two states. I don't!*

And James, always cool, sniffled and looked around a second before responding much more quietly than Warren had addressed him.

– *I don't believe I've ever seen you.*

James locked into his stare.

His stare was made even creepier by the obvious joy he contained, proud of the stinging comeback he was building up suspense for.

– *Of course there's lots of cars on the road like yours. All look the same. All perform the same.*

Two old cowboys with glasses on sat around outside the gas station.

A hand-painted sign read "Tire Bargains."

Warren sat back down in his car, his hillbilly music loud.

He watched the three of you.

*

James and you sat together on a fence next to the gas station, quiet for a while.

In the gentle lapping of the breeze, sitting quiet should've been such a treat after the long whistle and growl of driving, but James ruined it.

You were already irritable, uncoiling from those hours in the lumpy backseat and then James couldn't just relax.

He started pontificating about cicadas, the existential horror of their life cycles, the seventeen-year slumber to wake up to fuck, just so the next generation could hibernate seventeen years to do the same.

You couldn't even look at him until you finally had to cut him off.

– *You bore me.*

*

127

Leaving James sitting on that fence, you jumped in shotgun of the GTO.

Warren sat up, smiled and nodded, his eyes fixed on you.

You sat in silence except for the clicking of his tapes that you flipped through.

These are groovy records. – You finally said.

Play one.

You continued flipping, didn't look up.

You traveling with those guys? – He asked.

Yeah – you nodded. – *Say, where'd you get such a far-out car?*

Vegas. – He smiled big. – *I won it shooting craps. Thought I'd go to New York and spend some money. I don't care. I'm just gonna hang loose.*

That was before you knew he was a compulsive liar, but his slang sounded so forced, so clumsy in his mouth, it made everything he said ring phony.

He put on Kris Kristofferson's mournful version of "Me and Bobby McGee" before asking about The 55.

How fast does it go?

You both looked at it a moment.

He started getting worked up – *I could take him. I know I can.*

He jumped out of his car and marched over to The 55 to look it over.

It was obvious to you that he didn't even know what he was looking for, bending down behind the car.

The gas tank in the trunk stunned him.

James smiled to you, confident.

He whispered that it looked like you guys – *had a squirrel to run.*

Under a jumble of leafy trees a red hose coiled loosely through a broken fence.

Dennis talked Warren through putting his pink slip in an envelope to General Delivery Washington DC, told him – *Stay on country roads, less heat that way.*

And just like that, it was decided.

The marathon, the one you three had already been

immersed in, would be given some meaning, an ambition.

A race for pink slips.

Warren needed you guys.

Strangers meet and can occasionally lend each other meaning.

*

You didn't know what to call it then, but it was shame that chased you out of New York.

Back there, before hitting the road, you began to feel bad all the time and mostly you felt bad because you didn't feel worse.

You felt like you should've felt *very* bad because you weren't a Good Person.

You felt enough shame to end up marrying old gray-skinned Harry Dean only a couple years later.

You were still only learning to stand up straight when your mom died and your speech had only just become understandable, but somehow she taught you how to marry a man that much your senior.

Sometimes you wondered if you didn't stay with Harry Dean only because you couldn't stand to leave one more person.

*

And back in New York, you always thought of this other line from *The Bell Jar* because it also seemed so true: "If you expect nothing from anybody, you're never disappointed."

You had hurt people and you could conceptualize that.

But empathy didn't come simply to you.

When you thought about it, those people, the men back in New York, they weren't only as real as you, but *more* real.

The shock the men felt, it wasn't the shock of you leaving any of them, but the shock of the world being as it was and moving as it must, despite however anyone might've wished it otherwise.

LET GO AND GO ON AND ON

They were all like David Hemmings in *Blowup*, each one bossing the whole world around according to how it fits within his personal frame.

From within the cropped-framing of their limited little perspectives, the world – however it might appear to any one of the men from wherever he stood – the world had to be explained, squeezed, warped to fit, somehow, into the greater perspective of being all within his dominion.

And that's what disgusted you.

He, whichever man, his desires, domineered over The World: sometimes simply and modestly, sure, with grace and a smile, sure.

But still, always within his control.

He might've never even been able to name or articulate any desire until he witnessed that it had already taken shape.

And then, in its effect, diagnostically, he could recognize – "Oh, all along I must've wanted that. Such an outcome, how else could I have known what I wanted?"

But you leaving, that was beyond anyone's control, however many warnings you might've given.

Small plans shifted into little letdowns: that was practice for leaving that the men refused to see.

Ideologies contradicted in the most severe of terms, an ideological severing: practice for leaving.

You'd brush aside touches you'd previously leaned into.

Who wouldn't notice that?

The soft beat of his chewing, the weight of his snuggle, the wet mush of his kisses at the end: every time you looked at one of the men concentrating on a small task or he just smiled at you vacantly, unaware, every one of them you'd think the same thing – "he is just so ugly and stupid."

Trying to be nice, feeling ashamed, you'd explain little things away.

It's not you.
I'm just tired.
My stomach hurts.
Still, the thought of you with anyone else …

*

130

Until finally, no way it was worth it, hurting people, people you trusted conceptually to be *more* real than your experience of yourself.

The men, so confident in the solidity of themselves, each saw the world advancing as it did according to his own passive and self-satisfied commands.

Every one of them was always so goddamn sure.

It made you figure he must have some sense of himself in the world that you lacked.

He must.

All the men, they all knew something that you didn't.

Everyone did.

And so you submitted.

They all seemed to know.

And in that way they all seemed to you to be *more* real than you seemed to yourself.

All you had was your private island and your pet coyote.

And this was why you hated to hurt them.

It was why you feared that you should feel worse.

This is how you knew that were not a Good Person.

So you got drunk a lot.

You'd notice that you hadn't heard a word anyone had said in quite a while.

You'd realize that you hadn't stopped talking to take a breath in quite a while.

But didn't the men ever feel something wasn't right, even if they wanted it to be?

Wasn't it a jolt awake to admit that some things that you wanted to be true were really just beyond your control?

And actually, you knew it.

There are very few choices to make.

*

You sat in the stands in the sunshine and watched Harry Dean in the brutal pit.

Even outside, floating feathers tickled your nose.

It had gotten so just seeing the birds hop and flap around

in the scratchy green and brown of their pens began to make you gag.

Didn't even need the gore of the cockpit.

They're all white, gray or black, generally an ounce or two over five pounds.

You could tell with a glance if one mutant came in at a little more or less than that.

And you'd seen enough of them that they did eventually each look unique.

Two of Harry Dean's favorite birds became the quintessential specific chickens in your mind.

Every other bird you'd see was distinct in how closely it resembled one or the other of those two.

One, the top of its brown and bony beak was higher than its eyes and its frown at its beak's lowest back edges was at the height of its eyes.

Its eyes, solid black and reflecting the glare of a lamp like an inverse pupil, were so low on the side of its head, you doubted that it could even see forward.

Did only seeing sideways make it vulnerable to attack?

You never heard the men address that as an issue.

Its neck hung loose, vulnerable.

If it were a person, that neck would've hung from forehead to bellybutton.

All neck, all that skin with no muscle to fill it dangled like a deflated balloon.

Its back black over white with streaks of gray, like a suitcoat over its red neck and head, a dinner jacket worn up high on the back of its neck.

When at peace, it didn't look mean.

Dull and dumb, yes, but not violent, not like a killer.

In profile it looked like a dimwitted Cyclops bailiff taking his control over a court for granted.

Tired and blasé, his hours logged in the court were demonstrated through the deep wrinkles of his skin, the craggy blemishes of his beak.

Terrible hair, a few coarse pieces stood tall on top, the rest hanging flat and long in the back.

132

A bailiff, you could see silently eating his dinner on his lap: a dinner he had cooked on a hotplate, in his underwear in his dingy studio apartment.

A pale blue film covered his eyes when he blinked.

The other bird looked in perpetual shock with the white of its eyes opened wide, perfectly round.

Its eyes higher on its head, its hooked beak threatening, it panted through its open mouth.

Hanging its head like a winded basketball player having just chased an opponent's breakaway, its throat expanded and contracted dramatically.

The defendant, vitalized by desperation maybe, did always appear sharper than the bailiff, more alert.

"The Sport" the men called it.

*

But of course once the birds were set against each other, the gore of the cockpit worsened your nausea.

Feathers stuck to blood clumps.

Your stomach turned and head spun.

Relishing the applause, Harry Dean raised his hand in victory.

Bloody wrists at his white cuffs, he blew you a kiss.

But even as the applause continued, his expression changed.

His brow lowered.

His eyes darkened.

He marched right up to you, the exhausted chicken swinging behind him in one hand.

He shouted at you – *Why didn't you shoot that? Where was your camera?*

Shaken, the camera in your lap, you'd never picked it up, didn't think of it.

You said you took photos for Monte, not for him.

He twisted your arm pulling you down from the bleachers hard.

You were tempted to dare him to hit you, but didn't.

*

After a silent drive, you slumped into the dark motel room and Harry Dean apologized.

He glided along with the thrill of his big win, demonstrating his cheerfulness and needing you to share it with him.

He kept rambling on and on until arriving at some stupid truism or aphorism.

So if a man accepts life logically, the unexpected is actually the expected.

So proud of himself, he smiled big.

You shook your head and turned towards the bathroom to dismantle that day's red outfit.

He pulled you close and kissed you in big, sloppy kisses, panting heavily all at once.

You pushed him away, difficult to do with your arms bunched up against your chest in his embrace.

And finally it wasn't your force, but his willingness to accept your cues that released you.

With two long steps you went into the bathroom and closed the door behind you, one fluid motion.

He stomped around a minute before banging on the door and calling out.

– *Now you don't spend all night in that goddamn tub again you hear me? You think you're gonna melt in there? That what you want?*

You smudged your makeup off in the mirror, started the tub so its roar would cover his rant.

Still, faintly you could hear him shout at the door.

I've never known anyone to take so many goddamn baths!

*

Early afternoon in Chatanooga, you and Harry Dean stood around a motel room with a dozen men, all silent and a little confused, trying to eyeball the smallest details and imagine potential problematic scenarios.

134

A familiar bearded man in overalls, Warren's new partner, you thought, asked – *Who takes the risk for the room?*

His accent thick in his mouth, the organizer responded – *Course I take the risk.*

The bearded man in overalls nodded. – *But without the crowd you won't make your money to cover any damages.*

Shit. I know that. You think I don't know that?

The organizer looked to Harry Dean.

They all always looked to him, the elder statesmen.

He shrugged, shook his head, lowered it.

He sighed and loosened his tie, glancing to you at his side.

Holding your purse tightly against your chest, you were pressed back against a wall.

The organizer continued – *I thought you all men be appreciate I get some action at all for you, what with the sheriff and all.*

Harry Dean moved to the center of the room, waving his arm in a big sign of surrender. – *He's right.*

One man looked shocked. – *He what?*

He's right.

Harry Dean sure did love talking people into seeing his way. – *We all came a long way for this.*

And he sure did love being seen as the wise elder of The Sport. – *Better to make* something *happen than nothing at all.*

Nodding, the men all looked at their toes or the ceiling, or over each other's shoulders to the sparse afternoon parking lot.

No one said anything until the bearded man in overalls suggested with a sigh – *We can put the dead birds in the tub.*

Harry Dean looked to you.

You tilted up on your toes and felt the slight pull of muscles in your lower back.

You pinched your lips in at the corners a little and nodded in support.

He took your hand, happy to acknowledge your solidarity.

It was an implicit peace-making gesture after a morning of not saying much to each other.

The man who only a moment before had seemed cynical about the idea, tapped his knees and bounced in place a little. – *Alright then. Let's get them birds.*

I go hold the back door open for you all – the organizer offered.

Grumbling and shaking their heads, the men all exited the room.

Harry Dean smiled to you and, rolling his eyes, he threw his hands up in the air.

You smiled.

He threw his arm around your shoulder as you two stepped through the door.

*

When James and Dennis raced, both sides always handed the money over to a third party before the race even began.

The race wouldn't happen otherwise.

You didn't know why the cockfighters never thought to do that.

So entrenched in their ways, their codes of conduct that they all thought so gentlemanly, it didn't matter how many times Harry Dean had trouble with money.

You couldn't suggest that drag race business model, however much it seemed like common sense to you.

It just wasn't how things were done.

Of course, mostly you two traveled for tournament competition.

There'd usually be a couple dozen people there to watch.

Fifty people was a lot but not uncommon, often just a dozen people.

The big prize for the biggest single days might be around a grand.

But, if he'd been going through a dry spell, much as he hated to risk a chicken in a non-tournament fight, Harry Dean would often pick up what he could, sometimes one-on-one challenges for as little as twenty-five bucks.

Figured even twenty-five bucks, that's something: almost

the gas and the room for the day.

Some private hack, a hick with a warped-boarded barn splayed into shingles, would linger after a match and invite Harry Dean back to his farm.

And Harry Dean never knew what trick he might be walking into.

The pit might be slicked to give the local an advantage.

The local might stick his finger up the cock's ass to throw the fight, and the audience is all in on it and bets big against him.

Harry Dean's pretenses of sportsmanship and honor, exactly like Warren, it was all so stupid.

You saw your goddamn share of battles.

That's one thing you never needed to see again, a cockfight.

And you heard all about their sophisticated strategies.

Half the time those pit-chickens killed each other accidentally, each just kicking the other to try to untangle itself to escape the fight.

And every time Harry Dean won one of those pick-up fights, it always ended the same.

Always – *Gee, sorry.*

Always – *No cash on me now, but I'll just have to take down your address ...*

Warren always stood prepared to brawl if someone tried to run after placing a bet that they couldn't cover.

But Harry Dean, could you imagine him in his dandy Candy Land suit, twisting someone's arm back to dig through his pockets?

Nope.

*

And you had plenty of ideas about how Harry Dean dealt with money.

Of course you could never say anything.

A huge percentage of it was wasted on the costuming for both of you.

He really did dress like a Walt Disney pimp.

And that's what he thought of you in your Shirley Temple getups?

You had plenty of problems with how he dressed you up, and the money was the least of them.

But it was definitely an outsized expense.

You would've preferred maybe he saved something.

And really if he didn't occasionally indulge in such nice rooms after big wins, maybe you two could've afforded a little bit nicer standard of rooms day-to-day.

A couple times you did suggest that he had so much on his mind, maybe you could be of help keeping track of the money and making the budgets.

He laughed.

Things would've been a lot different.

At the very least he could've given you just a little bit of your own to carry around with you.

But it was a point of honor for him.

You had to ask him.

He had to pay for every little thing: a lipstick, a red cherry soda like Mr. Jimmy in your favorite song, tampons.

You could never ask him for bubble bath.

*

Pressed back, your head turned and cheek stuck to the motel room's sticky wallpaper, you held your breath and squinted tight to protect yourself from the feathers.

The squawks amplified by reflection in the small room.

The birds fought in the center of the room.

Hunched closely around them, on their knees and screaming, the men remained on the ready to untangle gaffs or claws from nylon carpet.

All this volume, shrieking loud, and the manic speed of standing so close up on the fight, it all unified into such a dense and immediate surface that no one noticed the boom of strange men kicking in the door.

Five of them, five men in rubber masks and suits stood all at once on top of the group, sticking wide-barreled shotguns up in your noses.

All the cockfighters jumped straight up, hands in the air.

The masked men fanned out, covered the room from the center, pushing everyone back to the walls.

Kicking the confused chickens aside, one masked man scooped up the pot.

Pressing the loose bills against his waist with the same hand that his gun awkwardly tilted in, he pulled the sheet off the bed with his other hand.

He threw the sheet to one side of the room, and everyone was quieted by its slow float, like a parachute.

He tossed the pot on the sheet, pinning it down quickly.

Gentlemen – this spokesman of the thieves began.

He looked around the room and seeing you, bowed with an overblown sense of manners. – *And lady. Please do as you are told and this will all be over quickly and no one will get hurt, OK?*

A couple men muttered *OK* and he continued. – *Now, keep quiet. Hold still and drop your pants.*

The men all glanced around to each other confused.

And the thieves gestured toward the men's belts, some poking at their buckles with the barrels of their guns.

The spokesman of the thieves waited a moment, surveying the room with a cool nod, before cracking open all at once into a scream, shouting – *I said drop your pants!*

The men all did as told, undid their belts or overalls, dropped them to their ankles.

Confused about dropping your red dress, flustered and scared, you pulled your panties off over your red knee-high boots.

That must've been scarier for you than anyone.

The thief watching you shook his rifle at your purse and you handed it to him.

One of the thieves scuttled around the room and picked up all the pants and tossed them over to the sheet.

The thief holding your purse tossed it to the sheet.

The spokesman thief looked around the room and nodded. – *Thank you all very much.*

He bent down and pulled up the corners of the sheet around their bounty and gripping it like a hobo's bundle, the thieves all filed out in a scurry.

It took a minute, a long silent minute, all remaining still, the pulse of the room's dirty wallpaper beating and the smallest feathers drifting in the sunbeams, before anyone, exhaling deeply one at a time, thought to drop their hands.

The bearded man in overalls finally started to laugh, looking around the room and pointing at each guy in his underwear.

A few of the other men began to chuckle too.

One man pulled a hefty wad of cash from the tobacco pouch in his shirt pocket.

He shook it and smiled and this was the weirdest part.

The door opened.

And how the thieves knew, none of you could even guess.

It seemed so unreal and silly, but one thief ducked back in, took the wad of cash from the man's hand and bolted out again.

*

Most mornings you'd be on the road by sunrise.

Each lingering night drifting into its next day, the days weren't so neatly divided as sleep means to distinguish them.

One morning, driving in silence, you saw sheep in fog on a hillside, everything blue.

I see the earth. It is so beautiful. – The cosmonaut said.

At night, Harry Dean would untuck his shirt, lie back in the bed and smoke, the smoke hanging thick in the yellow light of the nightstand lamps.

He insisted that even his undershirts be starched meticulous.

His complexion was splotchy shades of light gray.

In the next room, the running tub would drown out the clatter of the television: sirens and canned laughter.

Barnyard afternoons, Harry Dean would wave his clenched fists over his head in victory as on-lookers cheered.

You would clap politely, snap photos.

Mornings, if no particular subtopic of fighting birds

inspired a monologue, Harry Dean would usually sing as he drove: *Don't Be Cruel*, *All Shook Up*, *Heartbreak Hotel*, *Jailhouse Rock*.

To Harry Dean, Elvis represented a rebellion against country honky-tonk.

Seemed that you only ever had one song in your head those days: *You Can't Always Get What You Want*.

You liked to imagine that character Mick sings about, Mr. Jimmy.

You had a specific idea of what he must look like, but you just couldn't quite get it in focus.

That morning, that blue morning you saw sheep in fog on a hillside, you two drove in silence.

*

Back in New York, in the studio apartment that you shared with your friend the other model, in your oversized T-shirt, your knees pulled up tight to your chest, you would sit in a wooden chair at the shared desk, picking at your toenails.

Inhaling and exhaling deliberately, your friend the other model would lay on her bed smoking a cigarette, concentrating on the curling smoke in yellow lamplight.

Always dressed up back then, your friend the other model was going through a wearing-too-much-make-up phase, which you kept expecting to fizzle at any moment.

But it lingered and even continued to intensify, her long blond hair always put together just so.

You didn't hassle her about it.

I always know what people look like naked – she told you one time.

Oh yeah? Really? – You shook your bangs from your forehead.

People just look exactly like they do with their clothes on.

*

YOU CAN'T ALWAYS GET WHAT YOU WANT

*I went down to the Chelsea drugstore to get your
prescription filled.
I was standing in line with Mr. Jimmy and man, did he
look pretty ill.
We decided that we would have a soda, my favorite
flavor cherry red.
I sung my song to Mr. Jimmy and he said one word to
me, and that was 'dead.'*

*

I just think he's a phony – You told her, your friend the
other model. – *He is. He's such a phony.*

He's sweet. – she said emphatically.

You don't see through that?

You couldn't believe that someone that claimed to know
what everyone looked like naked, claimed to so easily see
through clothes, could somehow not see right through that
last guy's front.

What are you talking about?

He is such a phony. – You were bored with the conversation.

I think he's sweet.

You both sat quiet a second, before you pressed it – *And
he's dumb.*

He goes to Yale – your friend the other model replied
incredulously.

Doesn't mean he has any intuition.

*

First light brightened the dim violet room's thin curtains.

You pulled the blankets up over your head against the
morning.

Already up, getting dressed, Harry Dean yanked the
curtains open. – *It's almost five-thirty! Come on!*

He ripped the blankets off of you and you rolled over,

turned your back to his silhouette.

Which one of us are you trying to make a fool of? – He snarled, exasperated, with a pivot and a sigh.

– Because you know what, Cookie? People know about you. Everybody knows you're looking down your nose at them, so ain't no one gonna blame me. You aren't making a fool of me.

You sat up and grabbed the blanket, pulled it back up over yourself quick. – *Just let me sleep a little bit longer.*

I'll go without you. I don't care. I ain't too proud.

Good.

Good? You like that? Make a goddamned fool out of yourself with all your pouting like a little fucking Princess on parade.

You bolted up again, screamed loud as you could – *You parade me around!*

Lying back down, you ducked your head back under the blanket, muttered – *All the stupid red outfits.*

I parade you around? – He chuckled. – *Oh no Honey.*

He pulled the blanket off you again and threw it on the floor.

You rolled over on to your back and glared at him, his gray skin hanging from his feeble frame like a chicken's neck, his skinny wrists and his stupid loosely-looped, polka-dotted tie.

Rolling back over on your stomach, you buried your head under the pillow, embarrassed for him and embarrassed for yourself, knowing you were physically stronger than your old husband.

Fine, sweetheart. – He said.

He stepped over to the bathroom counter, picked up the wet clothes soaking in the laundry pot, and flung them at you.

They landed with a cold snap on your back.

You jumped up with a holler.

Maybe you can finally hang these to dry before I get back. – He shouted.

He pulled the door closed behind him hard, but its bang was muted, little more than a soft woof.

*

143

The motel rooms were all so the same, so familiar, each one with a torn up socket or the carpet knotted with glue.

And circling back around as you two always did, you didn't know how often you swore you'd been somewhere before that you hadn't, or you showed up somewhere Harry Dean insisted that you'd been before, and you didn't recognize it.

That whole day quiet, you spent the entire day lying on your side, just staring, falling in with the slow breath of the building through its vents.

You spread your collection of clippings out on the bed.

You hadn't looked at them in awhile: Paul Newman, Marianne Faithfull, Ike and Tina.

Finally, realizing you'd made it through to the other side of sunset, you got up only long enough to click on the radio then lay back down.

There was only country music or Christian news.

President Nixon spoke.

As we look to the future, the first essential is to begin healing the wounds of this Nation, to put the bitterness and divisions of the recent past behind us, and to rediscover those shared ideals that lie at the heart of our strength and unity as a great and as a free people.

By taking this action, I hope that I will have hastened the start of that process of healing which is so desperately needed in America.

I regret deeply any injuries that may have been done in the course of the events that led to this decision.

I would say only that if some of my Judgments were wrong, and some were wrong, they were made in what I believed at the time to be the best interest of the Nation.

You moved to the bath.

The tub was darker in some spots than others, but not dirty in any way that you could clean.

You didn't shave your legs.

*

The upkeep days, the behind-the-scenes and off-season days, Harry Dean would insist that you come along.

You'd visit farms with sheds of tin and wood stacked like villages of teepees.

Those days were even more boring than the tournament days.

Never a day off.

You were as far away from New York, further than you had ever meant to get.

Passing through some small downtown, early morning before the general store had even opened, your reflection on the grimy windows of the closed shops always taunted you.

Turning off on to some long road outside of town, marked only by the antlers on the mailbox or turn left at the tilting charred skeleton of the second burned-down barn.

You couldn't believe that the world could contain so many trucks abandoned to mud roadside long enough to become landmarks.

The entire middle of the country seemed to you to be rusted junk, sorted and stacked in like kinds and left in gravel lots.

Harry Dean would park up at the circle driveway near the house.

The smell of oil always hung thick in the country air.

Everything always in jagged pieces, big greasy bolts, and shredded belts left in the lawn that you always mistook for a garter snake at a glance, degrees of disrepair that were hard to guess, as you walked up on them if they were moving slowly towards unity or obliteration.

James Earl Jones's brother managed one network of those chicken farms.

You saw him around a lot.

He looked and sounded like a helium-balloon version of his brother.

Always considerate of your boredom, he'd often greet you and immediately point you towards a scenic hike through the trees or a stone path to follow over the hill to a lake – *Sit alongside it long enough, you'll swear its surface glare is a white field of light.*

He reminded you immediately of your dad or your brother, and Monte.

Of course Harry Dean didn't like you wandering off alone.

But you sure preferred it to watching the men kick the birds biting at their heels while they stood around talking.

Crooked legs like that, it'd need high-spurs to land anything. But it'll still miss more than it hits.

The men never missed an opportunity to validate each other with their truisms-in-common.

In The Sport, you're either in or you're out. It's all consuming.

*

By the time Harry Dean came back to the motel well after midnight, his movements broad and drunken, on display and proud, you had moved back to the bed from the bath, but had still never drifted off to sleep.

All day and all night you clung to wakefulness.

You wanted to enjoy every instant of silence and stillness that you could.

He came banging in, fell back on the bed pulling at his boots, landing on your ankle.

You scooted but made no sound.

Flopping down on his back, his coat still on even, he sighed loudly and pressed his palms hard to his eyes.

He remained silent a moment before you rolled over and, leaning up on an elbow, looked at him.

You stupid thing. – He said, rolling over on his side and pulling up against you. – *I bet you didn't eat all day.*

You pulled back a little, but not beyond his clumsy reach.

You had not done something stupid, not that day.

Couldn't think of the last time you didn't eat from a buffet.

Everyone smoked while eating.

Smoking helped you hide that you mostly just scooted the potato salads, gunky with mayo, around your plate, flattened the succotash and fanned it out to the edges, tore the fried chicken up but never tasted it.

You told Harry Dean, because you wanted him just to fall asleep, you said you weren't hungry.

And soon, still in his suit, his coat buttoned, shirt untucked and pulled up to his chest to cool his belly, his loud snore began.

And in his arms like soft chicken meat, you weren't even sleepy.

*

You sat in the backseat in the bright morning, massaging Harry Dean's shoulders while he drove.

He smiled big and you kissed him, doting little pecks on the cheek.

Now if its legs hang straight down when you pick him up from below, that's how you know. That is a good gamecock. – He said.

– It's gonna strike straight on and bring its head all the way back up, so when it comes down it's gonna have all that strength behind it.

You could be OK, long as you never arrived anywhere.

Driving, you always looked at him in profile.

You could do it.

Driving was OK.

*

At the motel that night you didn't say much of anything to each other, but smirked a good deal in passing, each of you content with the quiet.

He left you to your bath and you left him to the sirens, crashing through the wooden crates and rooftop chases of his cop shows on the television.

You fell asleep in a quiet and casual snuggle.

But late, around 3 AM or after, he was flipping over and rolling around so much, he woke you from a sound sleep like maybe he had intended to.

Putting your palm to his cheek, your voice soft as breath,

you asked – *Honey, why don't you sleep?*

I can't. – He said with a croak, clearing his throat.

Big day tomorrow. – You ran your fingers through his hair. – *Get some rest.*

He nodded, took a deep breath.

His tone serious, he said – *You know Sugar. You know I love you.*

You pulled up tight against his side and sighed. – *I know that.*

Why I love you like … I don't know. – He said. – *I just really do.*

You told him you loved him too and he seemed embarrassed. – *Yeah, yeah. I know.*

You scooted back and opened your eyes.

Looking at the space between you two – the space that he would appear in – you focused long enough that your pupils could open.

And slowly his shape faded into focus in the low light.

Touching his cheek, you gazed into his eyes and gave him a soft kiss.

You're gonna look just beautiful tomorrow night – he told you.

You said – *It'll be a nice dinner.*

You're gonna be the most beautiful woman there.

You're sweet.

I've been waiting six months to see you in that dress.

Big night. – You said.

Six months you'd been putting off putting on that dress.

He sighed.

You knew that you'd teeter over into wakefulness soon and then not be able to fall back asleep.

Everyone will be there. – He said.

Yep. – You agreed, rolling back over on to your back and closing your eyes.

You know everyone will be there? – He said.

I know. – You said and then you began to understand his nerves.

And then he said it.

Warren will be there. – He said.

You re-settled your weight, but didn't say anything.

I want you to apologize to him. – He said.

You sighed deeply, didn't mean to, but did.

You hear me? – Harry Dean's voice, especially loud in the darkness, became a little louder, firm.

I will. – You looked to him. – *I'll apologize.*

He nodded. – *It's not right and it was shameful.*

I know. – You agreed. – *I will.*

Well, alright. – He said.

Get some sleep – You told him.

You rolled back over and kissed him again.

Good night. – You said.

He said – *Good night.*

And you laid there awake pretending to sleep.

And you pretended not to know that Harry Dean lying awake next to you, also only pretended to sleep.

*

Like a castle, The Senator's mansion was set way back from the road far off in the fields.

You didn't know if you ever even caught The Senator's name.

Based on no greater authority than his own whim, hunch or bias, The Senator named The Cockfighter of The Year at his annual year-end tournament at Miltville.

Some years, if The Senator didn't see fit, the medal wasn't given to anyone.

You couldn't understand why the men all submitted to this power.

Each cocksman invited to Mitville got a room assigned to him at The Senator's mansion.

The Senator, courteous and aloof, was certainly conspicuous, there to be seen, but one did not approach him.

Everyone you had seen the entire season, all in the same place at once, all assembled for dinner under vast chandeliers the night before the tournament.

In ill-fitting suits, ruffled shirts under tuxes, each cockfight-er wore a printed number on his back, clumsy and stilted with put-on manners, chomping on gum to cover the hay on their breaths, chuckling uneasy to live up to some ideal of prestige.

Monte pulled you aside.

For the sake of The Championship he again upgraded your camera.

A blank piece of paper came out of the camera itself right as you shot it and a minute later the picture came into focus.

He demonstrated by getting a group, each with a wide gap between his or her front teeth, to put their arms around each other's waists.

All night Harry Dean got pulled this way and that, a handshake and a smile, his yellow teeth bright against his graying skin.

Smiling only made Harry Dean's eyes look even sadder.

And you kept your hand wrapped into his bent elbow, occasionally glimpsing Warren across the room.

And seeing him mingle in his homemade sign language, you couldn't believe that you'd never made the connection before, between him and the mimes from *Blowup* playing tennis.

*

And seeing Warren, it hit you.

In your head you heard the hurried first lines of that Kris Kristofferson song, "Lovin' Her was Easier (Than Anything I'll Ever Do Again.)"

I have seen the morning burning golden on the mountain in the skies.

Aching with the feeling of the freedom of an eagle when she flies.

You had to admit it.

You really had always wanted things to work out between you two so bad.

You just wanted to adopt him.

He had such a hard time in the world.

You thought that it was cute how tough he would act in

defiance of how sensitive he really was.

He was desperate to feel at home in the world.

And he felt balanced only when devoted completely to some radical eccentricity, like a vow of silence for example.

You could remember the exact moment that you first saw him at that gas station in the southwest.

And because you saw him that moment and that became a moment of consequence, you remembered the moment immediately before that.

Hypnotized by the zipping through slow hours and long miles, internalized and surrendered to that waking-dream state in which cause and effect swirled until blending, you'd been thinking, as if a premonition was preparing you to meet Warren, but you really had been laying there, bumping along considering the clouds, the tools digging into your back, distracted, all the cars you'd been in and out of that year, you remembered specifically thinking at just that exact moment – "really, I think I could love anyone."

It hit you.

At that moment you suddenly believed that the willingness to love was love's only necessary precondition.

Tenderness didn't question whom.

And then puffy-faced Warren's appearance only a second later felt like a dumb challenge issued from the depths of the cosmos itself – *Anyone, you say? Yes, him.*

And you were stupefied – *Him*?

But you had to wonder, though it was strange and scary for you to consider, if in actuality, it could've been that seeing him that first time, that first instant might've packed such a wallop that you instantly thought – "Him. I could love anyone."

The first sight of him might've compressed time in your memory, jumbled cause and effect.

*

Goddamn impossible Warren.

In every possible manner at every possible opportunity, he

chose to demonstrate how impossible he chose to be.

And yet, in his way, a way that you'd never known anyone else to possess, he was the smartest person you'd ever met.

He thrilled you with the connections he could make instantly.

He remembered everything he'd ever seen or read, and made brilliant, complicated connections simple and poetic.

His obsessive lying was only more evidence of his struggle to win control of his own mind.

And the vow of silence, that was proof of his front lines in the battle moving forward.

Both the hot-rodders and the cockfighters viewed sensitivity, any expression of it, as a weakness.

That must've also been the case wherever Warren came from, back there in Mansfield, Georgia.

And the challenge unique to the sensitive, was to cultivate this weakness into a strength.

That was Warren's defining struggle, even if he would never admit to it.

That kind of smarts, making connections, that took sensitivity.

Catching him glance at you across the floor of The Senator's party, his gaze aimed cautiously as you did remain on Harry Dean's arm, Warren looked at you concentrated, but indifferent.

Certainly not warm, and hardly familiar, he looked at you with curiosity, like an object he may have once had use for but could no longer exactly recall the function of.

You had promised Harry Dean you'd apologize.

You could only wait until the two men's eyes met and you on Harry Dean's arm would be marched over.

*

Conduct yourselves as ladies and gentlemen was the entirety of the rules for the audience that afternoon of the championship.

Its command was made more powerful by its vagueness.

152

And though you did indeed witness more ladies in attendance that afternoon than any other tournament of the season, it still seemed an extreme request for people drinking paper cups of soda, spiked or not, on bleachers hot enough in the sun to burn one's thighs, watching dumb chickens gore each other in the dirt.

Even the chicken coops made from clean, new wood were put together rickety and without pattern.

Harry Dean and Warren faced each other in the final round.

Each prepped his chicken in the far corners of the ring, the delicate procedure of tying on the gaffs such a funny contrast to the kinetic-carnage that it preceded.

Where others saw chickens, they both saw dollars and blood, which gaffs, according to how its legs hung and how long the neck.

They both liked looking at that thing, same as everyone else – a chicken – and seeing something different hidden right out there in the open.

They liked that their shared shifted-vision had a long history, a tradition that couldn't be parsed by an outsider, but had to be learned from within – an alternative history of a ubiquitous necessity, chickens.

They would recognize a fellow cocksmen on first sighting and they recognized the fools immediately too, coming around with nothing more than a strut and a dazed, untrained bird.

It was not only through battle, but through these recognizable signs, that Warren and Harry Dean each came to find his fiercest rival was the man he could relate to best.

Proud together, neither of them thought anyone else worthy to stand with them.

*

The instant camera Monte had given you the night before didn't interest you.

You preferred time in-between shooting and seeing the

photo.

It wasn't the object of the picture itself that you were drawn to, so much as seeing a moment that you had been in and being able to see it differently at a later date, in a different place.

It wasn't interesting to you to take a photo and look at it one minute later, as you sat in the same spot that you'd taken it.

You understood that this was *the* moment, the peak of the season, that if you were supposed to photograph anything it was this – The Championship.

But you just didn't care.

You couldn't get yourself to even lift the camera to look through it.

After some hours in the heat for the preliminary rounds you had walked back up to the room to change, as a *gentleman* should expect his perspiring *lady* to do.

Harry Dean not around to insist otherwise, you put on the green dress you'd never worn before, bought with the money Monte had paid you for your photographs.

Showing it to Harry Dean that day you bought it, he looked nervous, but said he liked its contrast to your red hair.

Swinging his chicken by its tail, standing on the precipice of The Championship match, silhouetted by strange flares of the sun off the dirt, must've been chicken-wire flat against the ground, Harry Dean looked up at you, alarmed, shocked.

The crowd anxious and dense, the man in front of you ate greasy and fragrant fried-chicken, licked at his fingers.

You squinted against the sun, fussed with trying to fix the slow folds of your sun-hat with a pin.

The two women you sat between had a conversation right through you.

They say it's the father-daughter combo you want.

No, no, no. It's the mother-son combo.

Instantly, Warren's bird kicked at Harry Dean's bird's head.

Some chickens so quick, could snap a neck between their legs, scissoring forward and back in a single leap.

Harry Dean's bird bit flesh from the back of Warren's

bird's neck.

You lost track of which bird was whose.

You knew Harry Dean thought you jinxed him wearing green.

You knew that he probably even thought that you intended to.

Right. – The women you sat between continued their conversation. – *The mother and son. You breed them and that's gonna get you a pit chicken with the biggest heart for fighting to the death.*

Right. Mother and son.

Blood on a white bird, the pit was a knee-high dust storm.

Everything so fast, it was all a drone.

Harry Dean took his eyes from the fight, leaned clumsy to wipe blood from his saddle shoes.

Right. Now that's what old Prometheus there is.

Right. But breeding, it ain't everything. This here might be the last fair contest in America, and breeding is a good start –

The gaff impaled through its skull poked straight out the other side of one chicken's head.

Which chicken was whose?

Solemnly, all the action quiet at once, both men squatted down low to look close.

Beyond the match, the grounds of The Senator's mansion were some Antebellum-dream, kinetic and layered, tumbling green and shocked clean wood in sunlight.

The expanse of it all popped against the sky, flat blue.

The referee between the two men moved down to one knee, closed the dead game-chicken's eyes; quite an exalted gesture of respect, you thought.

You'd seen Harry Dean like Warren and all of them, habitually, hundreds of times – any one of them would sometimes put a chicken's head in his mouth to comfort it.

And other times, any of them would tear a bird's head off with a yank, never thinking twice about doing that either.

*

PART 3

Annie Hall

(1977)

Far across the grounds, beyond the men hanging garlands on the palm trees, the caterer's people set up tables under a tent.

In the thick and tickling smell of fresh cut lawn, you worried a moment that your white jeans and white T-shirt might get stained green, the pollen drift of landscaping.

You hoped the caterers set up their tables upwind from the stables.

With a long slug from your tropical cocktail, one hand on your hip, you surveyed all of it, the perfectly groomed sprawl.

You didn't usually have a second cocktail before lunch, but the guests would begin to arrive in only a few hours.

No need to be nervous.

You were conscious of your own affectations; you felt at home within them.

Wearing your hair a little shorter, feathered, helped with the impression that you fit in.

Keeping your bangs still a little too long past your brow maintained your sense of continuous self.

You sauntered over, watched the people decorate the pool, the careful balancing of the floating bar with just the right number of bottles on each side of the inflatable Santa in sunglasses.

One chubby Mexican girl kneeling at the pool's edge, leaning, eventually insisted the younger white girl get undressed and jump in.

You smiled when they noticed you and paused.

They were nervous that you might offer a late-blooming opinion to contradict the efforts they'd already invested.

It really looks lovely. – You told them.

The chubby Mexican girl looked to the younger white girl, and the younger white girl smiled to you.

Thank you ma'am. – She said, squinting into the sun.

Her voice had both the twang and the throaty-quality that

you had been aware of shaking from your own voice since first arriving in LA.

Yeah, you bet. Great job. – You said, pitying her, her voice, her lumpy forehead.

You couldn't look at her, couldn't consider her any longer.

Turning, you bumped into a maid in a hurry, flustered carrying a basket of stacked white towels.

Oh. I'm sorry. – You said.

Oh no. Excuse me – she replied, visibly embarrassed.

It's OK. Are you OK?

Oh yes, yes. Fine, miss. Just need to get everything together.

The maid started to step away, but your thoughtful gaze obligated her to pause a second.

She squirmed.

You know, this place really looks beautiful today, doesn't it? – You said.

Yes ma'am.

You really did feel – it hit you sometimes, when you stopped to look, that you did live in some kind of dream– a young girl's dream of being a Princess.

Sometimes I just look out over all of it and I can't believe it.
It really is a very beautiful estate ma'am.
Isn't it?

You could sense her impatience to return to her work.

The maid said – *You are a very lucky woman, ma'am.*

You nodded thoughtfully.

You could see how people would think so.

Despite herself, the maid almost rolled her eyes, but instead said – *Excuse me then, ma'am.*

*

From behind, Paul hugged you around your waist and, moaning softly, you leaned back into the embrace.

Smiling, folding your cold drink in towards your wrist, you spun around into his arms.

He was in his mid-forties, almost a full head shorter than

you and balding, though his long combover really did look OK on him.

You tilted your cheek to the flesh of his scalp.

He wore his teal Hawaiian shirt open halfway to his navel.

When he growled playfully and bit at your shoulder, you touched your cold glass to his chest and he leapt. – *You win! You win! OK, don't!*

You two settled into a cuddle and stood still a moment together in silence.

Everything cool? – He asked.

You stretched away from him a little and sighed. – *Yeah.*

He pulled you close. – *Yeah?*

Yeah.

You sure there, Champ? You don't sound so great.

No, no. I just wish ...

He growled again and pulling your collar down, blew raspberries on your collarbone.

You pushed him away and he chuckled.

What? What? You wish what?

Nothing.

What? – He clasped your hands in his.

– *You are the beautiful young hostess of LA's hottest Christmas party.*

Yeah.

And I love you.

You sighed. – *I know.*

So what? – He bumped his nose to your chin.

– *What more could you possibly wish for?*

You looked over the grounds, the hedges at the fences far in the distance. – *Nothing, you're right. It's stupid.*

You pulled away and he pulled you back, kissed you on the cheek.

You wondered yourself why you were so needy *and* so bored.

You thought maybe you should consider volunteering.

Is that what the other women did?

I wish. – You said, not even sure that you meant it, or at least surprised to mean it if you did – *I wish it could just be us two sometimes.*

He looked shocked. – *What? Today? I throw this party every year.*

I know. I don't mean today.

Come on. You're just nervous. – He said smiling, his solution to everything: smiling.

Yeah, Maybe that's it. I'm nervous. – You said.

Of course that's it. – He said.

You set your head to his shoulder, stretching your neck uncomfortably to reach so low.

Now, you're going to be great. People are gonna love you, and it will just be a cool, mellow time. No big deal.

Lifting your head, you snorted. – *Four hundred guests is not 'no big deal.'*

You're gonna be great, OK?

He kissed you and stepped away.

I used to be smart. – You blurted.

Paul looked back at you, confused.

Squinting, he shook his head. – *What?*

Never mind. – You said.

You knew that you actually just used to be so dumb that you thought of yourself as smarter than you actually were.

In reality, you got smarter every day, realizing a little bit more, every day, just how much you didn't know, couldn't understand.

Paul turned to walk off again. – *I got some stuff to work out. Wanna go work out the set list. I gotta go, OK?*

OK. Yep.

People always insist on 'I Am a Rock' or 'Julio' at these things, and I've never played them with the new guy.

Yeah, yeah, do your thing.

You're beautiful, OK? People are going to love you OK? I love you.

You spun around and called out after your first step that you loved him too.

He walked off across the deck smiling, raising an arm, and calling out for a stage-tech to give him a hand.

*

Crossing through the few rooms to the kitchen, you smiled to the workers busy in each room, working: tacking down long cables to the stereo, setting platters of cold hors d'oeuvres aside in rows, balancing the bouquets, and setting folding chairs straight.

Your own big home, the one that'd taken you months to finally settle into, was once again being made strange.

In the kitchen, you pulled an egg and a package of raw hamburger meat from the refrigerator.

You forked the hamburger meat out into a bowl, cracked the egg on top of it.

You mixed it up with the fork and salted it, leaned on a stool at the counter to eat.

That was your comfort food.

The front page of the newspaper on the counter read: *As These First Consumer Computers Hit The Market, How Will Our Lives Be Changed?*

You stared at a photo of a man standing behind a computer with his arms open, as if presenting it.

You looked more and more closely at the photo until your vision drifted through the image and past it, reversed foreground and background.

It became only the dots of the printing process.

You could no longer see the image that all these dots were supposed to come together to form.

*

On the pill again, you had zits again for the first time in years.

But it was not a huge deal, even hosting a party, because keeping yourself clean and shaven and made-up was also simplified for the first time in some years.

You always wore all white with Paul.

Everything was always all white with Paul, some demonstration of the achievement of how easy a lifestyle could potentially be.

You would never spill anything.

And living there with Paul, your period gave you an excuse to get out of everything.

If you didn't feel like going to aerobics or meeting his friends for drinks, you could spend a night alone in the home theater wearing a mud mask.

Could you see it then, coming up ahead, that inevitable next indulgence: eventually letting yourself go?

*

But still, even just within the big estate, you were always looking straight ahead, never stopping in any one place.

Your cocktail steadied under your arm, you wandered from room to room, nibbling from your bowl of raw egg cracked over raw hamburger meat, enjoying its slow melt in your mouth.

You paused in the doorway of one of the living rooms; the one with a long leather couch wrapped around three of its walls.

Jeff Goldblum sat on the couch, leaning forward and cutting a line of cocaine on the glass coffee table.

He had always reminded you of your dad or your brother or Monte, and James Earl Jones's brother.

You liked Jeff immediately.

He muttered to himself under his breath, repeating something over and over like some kind of mantra.

Noticing you, he offered you a line with a wave.

You shrugged and walked over and sat and smiled.

Probably wouldn't hurt, having already had a couple drinks before all the other guests arrived.

You set your drink and the bowl down on the table. – *Thanks, Jeff.*

No problemo, for the lady of the house. – He said.

Wiping your bangs from the table as you leaned down, trying to get them to stick behind your ears so they wouldn't sweep away the line, you saw Jeff reflected in the tabletop's glass.

Poking at your bowl with the fork, keeping up his mantra

the entire time, he curled his lip in disgust.

*

Your modeling coach back in New York had this amazing office.

So many plants, just green everywhere and faded beige.

She only ever called you in to scold you.

You never imagined someday missing her or that humid room.

Even when obviously worn down, she spoke with a keen-edged tone.

– *Were you aware the scholarship deadline was last Tuesday?*

You had to be honest, shook your head no.

So am I to assume that you're almost done with the application?

But the office was so amazing, so dense with plants, you didn't mind going even though you knew it would mean a scolding.

I haven't started it yet. – You admitted.

The modeling coach readjusted her weight in her seat. – *Laurie, I called in quite a few favors for them to guarantee me that you are in, if you would just complete the paperwork.*

I know.

You don't appreciate my effort?

No. I do. – You said.

The modeling coach sighed, sat up taller in her seat. – *Well then, why have you let this slip? If you are afraid that it'll interrupt your career –*

It's not that.

They understand the circumstances and are more than willing to accommodate –

It's not that. I don't care about that.

So you don't care about modeling and *you don't care about your scholarship?*

She intensified her stare. – *Everything is just fine and you just don't care.*

165

You considered the thickness of the leaves of two different plants, both equally dark, dark green.

But one plant's leaves were thicker, didn't fan out so much.

We had a good time when we first met, right?

You nodded. – *Yeah, guess so.*

You reminded me of myself at your age.

You used to tell me that. Yeah, thanks.

You told me you wanted to go to school and then travel Europe and then you wanted to write books of poetry, maybe return to the States to settle down and teach at a small college. You remember all this?

You nodded. – *Mm-hmm, yep.*

That was your plan.

Mm-hmm.

Modeling was going to pay for everything it'd take to get you on your way, so you could see your plans through. Remember?

Yeah.

So what about your plan? You can't lose focus on your plan.

You started – *Yeah, but* – and decided to find a cigarette in your purse.

The matches were deep in your pocket, the other pocket than you thought and that pocket was pinched tight by the way your weight was set on the chair.

You knew that the modeling coach always liked you because like in *The Bell Jar*, when they asked you what you wanted to be, you wanted to be everything.

You took a slow drag from your cigarette, exhaled before speaking.

– *Maybe I feel like …*

Yes?

I don't know, it's like … my plan, as you state it back to me, all these opportunities I appreciate very much, but …

But what?

But like, I can tell you exactly what I think I want to do and you can repeat it back to me word for word, right?

Yes.

166

But however ideal it ever seemed, now it all seems so rehearsed, the sound of the words when I spell out my plan – Europe and poetry and whatever. It's all so much the same every time, that it's all become the last thing in the world I feel like I'd ever want to do.

Your modeling coach shook her head. – *But we've been working together to make the plan happen exactly as you always said you wanted it to happen.*

I know. Thank you. It just all seems so unreal now.

It was all unreal before and we've both worked very hard to make it all very, very real now.

*

You stood alone in the front hall, the house crowded and continuing to fill up, the stream of people unbelievably never thinning.

Turns out you could remain in one place just so long as a room appeared to zoom towards you.

You would duck back a minute at a time, hide behind your bangs to catch your breath, muster the will, then project: greet and make each person who entered feel special and welcome.

– *Oh yeah. The bars are over there and over there, and if you're hungry there's a spread in the yard just outside the East doors.*

A quick moment mid-spin between hellos, you looked over to Paul across the room, and admired the ease with which his steady mellow tone could float between conversations.

– *You should see Angelica pick on Jack while he plays. You don't need to be shy at all. I mean, his game is really good and still she just picks on him.*

*

He'd never admit it, but you knew how Paul despised people without money.

In fact, he'd be shocked and offended to hear such a claim.

He flattered himself such an empathic humanitarian, with his condescending appreciation of the soily people he might come across when they trimmed his landscaping or cleaned up after his spill at a restaurant.

But even being friendly to those that he saw as "other," even that was a manner of flattering himself.

It wasn't racism.

You would never call it that.

South African music and zydeco were the only records he'd ever listen to besides his own.

He had a curiosity about race.

His thing was obviously all about money, not skin tone.

And insecurity didn't motivate it.

It wasn't that he feared or could ever even imagine being bumped from his exceptional prestige.

It was stranger.

He had no choice.

It was systemic, practically beyond his control.

You had never known anyone more self-satisfied, which was not to say Paul was overbearing.

He was comfortable with himself, and when he did accept people, he accepted them easily and with warm welcome.

But he knew how to recognize at a glance who he would accept or not: the stitching of a handbag or sweat suit, the swoop cut into a heeled leather boot, the color of the label on a bottle of Scotch.

He knew precisely whom he was supposed to know and they all knew how to communicate it to each other through codes out in the open that only the worthy would even recognize as coded.

A pun might quickly determine, did this guy know the rules to handball as played at one exclusive club or not.

And you weren't naïve.

You knew that part of why you turned him on so much was how you were excluded from these codes.

In his mind, this exclusion kept things simple between you two.

*

The party's population density peaked by late afternoon, everyone so squashed, one more mustache wouldn't fit in the house.

Tony Roberts and Woody Allen stood next to the waist-high gong at the door, unable to even enter the party.

But they seemed content to be awkward on the sidelines.

Plenty of the guests wore their sunglasses inside.

Wide beams of light were thrown and reflected above in the angles of the two-story-tall ceilings.

The LA weather so perfect, even on Christmas, one guy you chatted with wore a corduroy coat over a turtleneck sweater, and his date wore just a light shoulder-less floral blouse.

That's how perfect the weather in LA was – it was whatever anyone wanted it to be.

With the exception of a few conspicuously young dates on the elbows of rich, leather-tanned divorcees, everyone was a lot older than you.

You were twenty-four then, but everyone else was at least thirty-five, forty-five not uncommon.

But you had even less to say to the other young girls than you did to the other guests.

You felt embarrassed to potentially be mistaken for one of them.

You were as far away from Long Island as you could get and still be in the same country, and that's what you had always wanted.

Dee Dee, your frumpy old friend from back home, had been in LA a couple months earlier, and you didn't know how she'd managed to track you down, but you ignored the message.

It must've been meaningful somehow to at least appear unreachable.

*

A notion becomes a concept becomes an idea.
You delighted in untangling overheard small talk.
And you talked with your hands, even learned to touch

people when you spoke with them, a light hand to their shoulder or elbow.

It had taken you no time at all to move through the initial shame and awe that came with Paul's Pygmalion plan for you.

And there was a utopianism to LA's class system, anyone could be redeemed or made clean by the all-powerful spectacle.

*

You approached Tony Roberts and Woody Allen to welcome them.

Tony had just moved to LA and was starring on some new big hit sitcom, the kind of show that had an immoral amount of canned laughs.

You had never seen more than a second of it, but it was a big enough deal that everyone would recognize him.

Woody Allen, his top button buttoned tight under a tweed coat with jeans greeted you first. – *Hi.*

Hi. You're Woody Allen, right? – You said.

Why yes. Yes, hello. – He said.

He seemed extremely nervous, sick with nerves.

Do you live around here?

No. No. I'm just in town for some shock therapy, but unfortunately there's this power crisis.

That's funny. – You said, even though it wasn't so much the joke that was funny as much as it was funny that he thought to tell such a corny joke.

He squirmed a little. – *Yeah. Oh, this is Tony Roberts.* – He said gesturing to his friend.

How do you do? – Tony said, nibbling nuts he pulled from his coat pocket while he spoke.

And you said hi.

You shook hands.

He's my food taster. – Woody Allen said.

Oh, he tastes the food to make sure it's not poisoned. – You said, nodding, realizing a second too late that you should've smiled. – *That's funny.*

170

Yeah. Well. – Woody Allen kept squirming.

He could probably tell that you didn't really think that was too funny.

Your own home made strange with guests, you froze.

You couldn't summon one more fleck of a thing to say to one more person you didn't really know.

Needed to throw another drink down quick.

Tony Roberts had a beard that his character on TV didn't have.

Both men fidgeted a bit, the pause in conversation becoming noticeable.

You wanted to tell them – *No, I'm not really like this.*

You could talk to any of those people there, any single one of them on their own.

It was just the sheer bulk of them at once.

It was just the pressure of hosting.

Hosting making you self-conscious, being self-conscious making you drink more, drinking more making you more self-conscious, which made you over-explain everything.

You looked Tony Roberts and Woody Allen over for a moment from behind your bangs.

You knew you were doing it and didn't want to, but couldn't help it.

You guys are wearing white. It must be in the stars. – Woody Allen said. – *Uri Geller must be on the premises someplace.*

The tiny copper buttons on your jeans matched your hair.

All white. – You said. – *Guess so.*

Muted sexiness was your unstated but understood agreement with Paul.

You were to appear always sexy, but never conspicuously so.

But the all white was just awkward, your panty line always in the back of your mind.

Woody Allen rolled his eyes to you when Tony Roberts said, as if you were just another of what must appear to him as an endless stream of Playboy Bunnies – *We're going to operate together.*

And yeah, you bet not only was Tony Roberts not ashamed of the hammy canned laughter on his show, you bet he sat and directed the sound-effects guy about how much laughter and what kind when.

Mistletoe hung from stacked popcorn cans.

Among the fruit piled in a tower on the buffet table, mirrored pedestals under a heavy red tablecloth, Santa stood, the same size as the sliced ham in its hotplate.

*

Most days, alone in the giant house, you were fine sitting around.

You must've been shocked to realize that at some fundamental level it was really no different than your years of drifting.

The perpetual surprise of restlessness: really, still no charge, no obligation?

One moment to the next: the small shock, the meaninglessness of each singular action.

– *I'll get a drink of water: turn on the tap, hold the glass.*

– *Oh, I'll look out that other window again: walk across the hall, open the curtain, lean.*

– *Oh, I'll flip through this book, never get lost in it, but flip.*

And so what's the difference?

– *Oh, I'll get in this car*

Or

– *Oh, I'll stay seated on this tree stump*

Or

– *Oh, I'll host this party*

Or

– *Oh, I'll just lay back in this bath?*

But you had come to expect bathtubs to be cleaner.

And it surprised you that it used to never even occur to you that they were occasionally truly filthy.

*

Your mom died when you were three.

Your father, he never did completely expel the Navy from his ways.

And by association, perhaps he assumed you all, his children, had all enlisted.

And your mother's sickness, ovarian cancer, and then her death, he took all that as a personal insult.

His pride, that man, so stern, he kept you all off-balance.

You learned to walk like a cat, balanced even with all your weight thrown to one side, strutting under obstructed headroom.

And he felt Ovarian Cancer itself had set out against him, to belittle him personally and deny him his primary attendant, your mom.

And, you supposed, maybe stupid as his resentment at the whole universe always seemed to you, maybe you too had somehow picked up a version of his idea.

You thought maybe her impulse to escape him was so deep-rooted that she had to get away in whatever way she could.

You could never say that.

But it sure did feel true sometimes.

And the world as a whole, the sum of its immersions, it just never could keep secrets well.

Sometimes it seemed to you that all anyone ever does is struggle to keep buried all the secrets that the world is trying to tell.

And it's not exactly dishonesty or even fear that keeps people from hearing.

But it might be just somehow impossible for people to comprehend how we've all ended up where we each do.

Weren't you once surprised to find yourself waiting for the sun to come up in the chill of an all-night diner's parking lot, no cars passing?

*

And it – all of it – required the expending of your reserves of quiet, but you'd spent all of the quiet that you'd been able to save up.

You'd been prudent, didn't squander it once you'd recognized its necessity.

Achieving any sustained degree of quiet, you always attempted to remain within it to fortify yourself.

And that was easy enough for you to do, to stay within, because that had always been your default bias anyways.

But even you, you who knew and respected the quiet's necessity and you who recognized its potential, even for you it was easy to get distracted by the noise – much easier than *not* getting distracted by the noise.

Like Plath writes in your beloved *Bell Jar*: "I took a deep breath and listened to the old brag of my heart. I am, I am, I am."

But the men were always all bluster.

Young men: James Taylor and Dennis Wilson; older men: Warren Oates and Harry Dean Stanton.

Men with money: Paul Simon.

They all liked to look at you, wanted to touch you, and that did give you some degree of power.

They liked how you looked and they liked how you felt, your skin.

Your power depended on gauging the exact proper distance to keep, just out of reach, but close enough to get a whiff, a glancing fingertip against.

That was all you had to learn to get what you wanted, that proper distance.

And your mom had lost perspective on that.

She let him overwhelm her.

What did she know?

Long Island was a long way from Manhattan.

That sweethearted thick-skulled Navy-Ass with his deep sense of correct etiquette, she allowed him to overwhelm her.

Maybe she even romanticized that he was overbearing only in the most tender of manners.

But working long hours never tired him enough.

He had a sense of self in the order of the universe that

needed balancing.

If his foreman or the men in the office took anything out on him, it'd get passed down to all of you.

You'd hope for him to be quiet and then when he'd come home quiet, you'd wait for something, any little thing, to set him off.

And just as he had that balance to keep, so too Mom had that balance to keep.

So she played it out the only way she could: to the fullest extent of the limited power she had, between herself and him.

She had failed to keep the proper distance.

And to make up for this would require a single, impossibly large gesture: the largest any gesture could get, a gesture the full-expanse of the universe could not contain.

She *chose* to die of ovarian cancer and you knew it.

And you couldn't blame her.

How else, what smaller action could've ever reset the balance to keep him uneasy, regretful, mourning and lamenting her?

*

 You slipped into the bathroom and closed the door on the party, sat down on the closed toilet and dropped your head in your hands.

You considered maybe taking a shower.

You'd never stepped into the shower in that bathroom before.

Leaning, remaining seated, you pulled the handle and the stream was sudden against the curtain, loud like hard rain on a car's thin sheet metal roof.

You took a few deep breaths before taking a really deep breath.

You stood and took a Valium from the medicine cabinet and swallowed it with water.

It felt good to dangle your hand under cold water a second.

It felt like maybe only your hand under the water had any

sense, the rest of your body felt acutely numb in comparison.

The medicine chest open, you glanced up, pulled out a razor blade and inspected it, holding the edge up closely to your eye to consider its sharpness close-up, its chinks and glitches.

Holding it up so close, you couldn't help but imagine it slicing across your eye, the goo or blob that'd pop from the compromise of its form.

And your vision, really, in material-form, it was made up of nothing more than the strategic collaboration of blood and light?

You rattled a big bottle of pills, poured them out spilling over your cupped hand.

You collected them all one by one, their outer edges beginning to melt against the drips of water in the sink.

You placed them carefully one by one back into the bottle.

*

That panicky feeling wasn't entirely new to you, but it'd been a while.

It was more like the rattling chain return of an identifiable phantom than some looming mysterious-unnamable.

First time, you remembered, under the lights in the photo studio, your friend the other model moved in a slow and clunky counter-rhythm to the flashes and the high energy of the crew.

You stood at the hospitality table and stuffed whole, rolled-up deli slices into your mouth, absent-mindedly absorbed in your friend's gestures.

The record had ended.

There was a moment of quiet while an assistant moved to put on the next record.

As always, the photographer hummed to himself, between his nonsense chatter. – *Lotsa smiles. Lotsa energy. High energy. Uh-huh-ba-da-bum-ba-da.*

But these small compulsive sounds of his now seemed loud in the room.

176

And *professional* that she was, or was at least becoming, your friend the other model fell gracefully into the required zone.

Watching her, all at once you hit a tipping point, something flipped, and then falling, accelerating, you just couldn't look, couldn't stand to watch her.

She appeared to you stripped of all culture.

A muscular beast, majestic and terrifying.

Sinewy and radiant, her every twist balletic, she appeared luminous and ancient, like some deer hopping lightly and happily, its antlers a crown of flames.

She did not appear to you *like* that flaming deer, but *as* that flaming deer.

You knew it to be eternal, but knew also that you weren't supposed to see it.

Witnessing it terrified you – it: The Wonder.

Without tempering or filters, how could anyone not be overwhelmed and exhausted by the constant elegance, the perfection of every small gesture?

Yet she, your friend the other model, for the sake of the fake David Hemming's humming orders and for capital, she squashed her innumerable variations into clichéd choreography, like some cloud stuffed into a small cardboard box.

You leaned back against the wall and closed your eyes.

But it wasn't enough to escape the flashing of the bulbs, darkness popping brown and pink.

Your collar tight or your throat clenching, felt like someone sitting on your chest, you couldn't breathe deeply enough.

The photographer's babble – *That's perfect. You got it. That's it. You're perfect.*

You stepped out into the concrete stairwell.

The thump of the heavy door echoed loudly; the click of its clasping shut, small punctuation.

Hands to the railing to twist your back, your forehead hot and your cheeks hot too, you felt like something choking you.

Your collar cinching, you gasped for breath, a moan to swallow a howl.

*

You and Paul led Woody Allen and his girlfriend, Diane, through a slow, sauntering tour of the house.

You could tell Paul liked Diane.

They'd stop to chat each time they came up on another one of his gold records hanging on a wall.

Seemed like maybe they'd met before or already knew each other.

Oh yeah, it's great. – Paul said – *A sauna, a Jacuzzi, three tennis courts.*

Didn't he have any idea how obnoxious he sounded bragging?

Diane tugged at Woody Allen's elbow. – *Oh wow.*

Oh yeah. – Paul went on. – *And then guess who he sold it to?*

Who? – Diane asked.

Like Warren's practiced speech about the GTO and Harry Dean's Cock-Truisms, you'd heard Paul's speech about the house a million times.

He performed it for you first time you had come over, verbatim.

And that time, hearing it the first time, his self-satisfied hot air didn't clang so much.

It seemed then, to you, like he was excited about it, couldn't believe his own luck, which in a way spoke to his modesty – that he wouldn't feel entitled to such opulence.

But with the speech now memorized, maybe he'd gotten lazy in performing it, or maybe you had come to recognize the intentionality of the production.

But it was still repulsive.

Charlie Chaplin – Paul announced, annunciating each syllable dramatically, staring at Diane for a reaction. – *Right before his un-American thing.*

My god. – Diane responded, hushed with awe.

Satisfied, Paul nodded – *Yeah.*

Diane looked to Woody Allen. *Yeah. That's something.* –

He said, shrugging.

Woody Allen looked really about to flip out, whether it was the suckering of Diane or what, whatever.

He wasn't having it.

*

At the doorway to the screening room, Paul halted the group amble.

You didn't like the look Woody Allen gave a couple of your guests sprawled out on the couches.

His nose pinched a little as if he were sniffing the room.

That Rolling Stones song "100 Years Ago" was playing.

Diane said something about how clean LA was, which seemed awkward to you in a way that however much you were irritated with the conversation, you thought you'd all at least gotten beyond that degree of small talk.

But you could hardly make out what she said over Woody Allen's condescending sneer as he eyed the screening room.

We saw Grand Illusion *here last night.* – You said, proud that yes, you did live in a mansion with your own home-theater.

With your hand in his, Paul nodded at you like you were his adored child.

But it didn't bother you like it sometimes did.

Woody Allen shrugged, unimpressed, and one of the guests flopped on a couch, without looking up, said – *That's a great movie when you're high.*

And he was right, you thought.

It is.

Jean Gabin and Pierre Fresnay are French soldiers in WWI.

Erich Von Stronheim, a German soldier, shoots down their plane and then invites them to a nice lunch.

The rich guys, Pierre and Erich, both captains of course, figure out that they have some friends in common and the Germans even observe a moment of silence upon hearing of a French soldier's death.

Jean and Pierre are put in a sort of dorm room with some

other soldiers, and they all cook nice meals together.

They're digging a hole to escape.

They expect to come out beyond the far buildings and up into the garden.

When down digging this tunnel, Julien Carette, who used to be a theater guy and is still always silly, he pulls the alarm to say he was suffocating.

You weren't sure why, what kind of fumes would've been under the soil in Germany in the 1930s?

But no one noticed the alarm.

And it's so weird.

All the French POW's are playful in the German work camp.

They have sing-a-longs and they make up dances together.

They revel sensuously in their most-prized contraband: dresses and wide swaths of uncut silk.

When one guy gets all dolled up, they all fall silent.

They all make up a dance routine together in drag, big kicks and wigs, waving big fans and singing falsetto.

It's so weird, but you liked how it was made.

They do this thing with the newspapers to show developments in the war without having to cut to life outside of camp.

When Jean bottoms out in solitary, the guard gives him a harmonica and some cigarettes, lingers by the door to listen to his mournful harmonica-song.

When it comes time to escape through the hole, Pierre with his upper-class monocle, he would've left Jean behind.

But then they all get moved to another camp that day right before the escape and Jean tries to tell the incoming prisoners, British officers, about the tunnel, but because of the language barrier he can't.

You did like the movie a lot, but after that part you were drifting in and out of sleep and lost track of what happened.

*

And that pipsqueak asshole Woody Allen just stared at you like maybe he just spit up his lunch.

Diane smiled politely but condescending, at you, blank eyes.

You knew the look.

Diane was wondering, trying to figure it out like a math equation, because she really couldn't tell: were you more or less pretty than her?

Were you maybe even beautiful, maybe even beautiful in whatever androgynous manner Diane attempted to affect with her stupid ill-fitting men's suits?

We've got six beautiful horses. – You announced, defensive for Paul as much as yourself.

You really didn't like this Woody Allen guy at all, his patronizing looks like all you and Paul did was eat and watch movies all day.

Paul, attempting to move the group away from the screening room, smiled at you as he pulled at your wrist.

That's all I ever wanted as a kid. – You said. – *To you know, to ride a horse.*

But, how about you two? – Paul turned to your guests. – *Still New Yorkers?*

Woody Allen said – *I love it.*

And Paul started to drift through the rooms again, pulling the rest of you along with him.

He does. – Diane said. – *He really loves it there.*

Oh yeah. I lived there for years, but you know ... – Paul said, with an almost pitying tone.

No. What? – Woody Allen looked defensive.

The city. – Paul made an effort of appearing to choose his words carefully, not wanting to offend. – *It's just so dirty there now.*

Woody Allen turned to walk off.

I'm into garbage. – He said, rolling his eyes to you. – *That's my thing.*

Come see our bedroom. – Paul said, and that was a weird thing to say, you thought.

These people didn't need to see your bedroom.

*

Paul was at ease with The Good Life.

But personally, you always found Struggle attractive.

And not in the easy or passive sense of the word "attractive," but "attractive" in the most literal sense: drawn to – you looked and then you had to look again.

You were *attracted* to Struggle because it was what you could understand.

And you understood that that was why you were attracted to it and how you were attracted to it, but you also understood that that awareness didn't make you immune to it.

How much simpler a life, to not be attracted to Struggle?

And no one you had ever known had ever struggled like Warren.

Everything was a performance for him, and every performance was a search for some abstract sense he had of his true self.

He had some notion, he'd never admit it, but his struggle was proof – he had some notion of some True Self that he would someday arrive at, like this True Self was a location.

Some ends.

What you saw in him and recognized of yourself in him, was that his *true* True Self was in actuality this constant struggle to arrive at this place that he mistook for his True Self, this place that he could never recognize until he found himself there.

You knew that he in fact remained there, always, because Struggle itself *was* the True Self.

At least you knew that was true for you.

When you felt easy in the world, it was only when you felt easy with constant struggle.

And in some past life Warren had been burned.

Back when he used to talk, he talked about everything that had fallen apart – *It All Fell Apart* – everything he had believed in, been taught to believe in, and never questioned.

It wasn't until he settled into what he assumed to be his life and that all fell apart around him that his life really began.

And in this life forced upon him, endlessly lost, his True Self could emerge.

So, who did he miss every day, who from his past life?

You couldn't say – a wife, some idealized small town beauty queen, you guessed maybe a little kid somewhere.

A little kid who wouldn't know him, but Warren would recognize by its eyes.

A wife and a little kid that he probably found no fault with, but only longed for simply and felt undeserving of.

And so his perpetual challenge became to prove his own worthiness of winning them back – the GTO, the always being put-together-perfectly, the best of everything; music collection, bourbons, cheeses; and then the competition, The Sport, the championship worth vowing muteness for.

You knew his denim outfits worn so casual were just one more ideal of being put together perfectly.

The standard of perfection, perfectionism, it's the self-loather and the regretter's perfect device.

Never being able to live up to an unattainable ideal offers constant reinforcement of one's own faults.

Brooding justified.

The sharpness of attitude and sneer at others: justified.

And then the flashes of success, seldom and sudden, brief as they might be, justify the mania.

Elated beyond any sense of self-control, blown beyond the constraints of identity, at one with the universe, if only for a moment the universe itself is justified because The Perfect has been achieved.

Of course the highs only make the crash landings harder.

But it's the crashes that matter.

It's the crashes that confirm one's lowliness.

This unworthiness, the constant seeking of new variations and models through which to play out its rituals, all bloom from that single crooked shoot, the cracking open of the world when *It All Fell Apart*.

And who could resist loving that: Struggle?

Anyone would want to help, right?

No one could be cold enough, so unfeeling as to pass by and not want to help.

You understood.

Everyone understands pain, knows to recoil.

You can't pass by someone sinking in quicksand and not offer a branch.

And, yes, it might be a harsh comparison, but that was the attraction – that attraction, the compulsion to help that one feels when passing someone being sucked down into quicksand, the earth swallowing them.

And it was love, not just because you wanted to be needed.

It was not just some lack of meaning in your own life that offering help could supplement.

But it was love because love was what was asked of you, required of you.

Maybe understanding him did require you to adopt some truisms, generalizations you most often hoped to avoid.

But who could deny someone sinking in quicksand whatever small thing they might ask of you?

And in return, maybe it would benefit you as well.

Negate all that *self* that oppressed you.

*

WILD HORSES

Childhood living is easy to do.
The things you wanted, I bought them for you.
Graceless lady you know who I am.
You know I can't let you slide through my hands.
I watched you suffer a dull aching pain.
Now you decided to show me the same.
No sweeping exits or off stage lines.
Could make me feel bitter or treat you unkind.
I know I've dreamed you a sin and a lie.
I have my freedom but I don't have much time.
Faith has been broken tears must be cried.
Let's do some living after we die.

*

Jostling through elbows, your paper plate wobbling awkwardly, you moved to nibble directly from the serving dishes.

You drank white wine all afternoon.

Greeting every person you'd never seen before or had met before but didn't remember or remembered meeting before but had to reintroduce yourself to, nonstop all day, and something had come free in your mind.

You had cracked open.

And while you were cool and easy playing the charming hostess, Paul had ample opportunity to lavish his attention upon whatever specific guest he may have deemed worthy, i.e.: Diane.

You were young, seventeen, still a kid, when Warren first prepared you, or his image of himself you should say, with his chinos and ascots, racing his dandy GTO; how it prepared you.

You got a quick sense of men around middle age and their fears, fear's power to warp.

And Harry Dean's industry fame, his success within The Sport couldn't be exceeded.

He'd reached the ceiling, sure.

Older men, yes, and successful, sure in a way, but neither of those guys was famous.

Not like Paul, Paul was *famous*-famous.

He was like a person that people thought of as a star, beyond his specific talent or field, magnetizing in whatever context.

People gravitated toward him, in a coffee shop, at the basketball game – his seats on the floor right behind the bench distracting the players – wherever.

That was part of being with him.

Time slowed in the flashes of cameras and breaths held wherever he went.

You two dealt with it when it happened, but it never came

up between you.

And the one thing you two really never talked about was The Money.

Of course it was The Money that allowed you everything – your entire lives, lifestyles, were buttressed by it.

It was the soil that nourished all that you two rooted yourselves in.

After drifting – the marathon with Dennis and James you didn't even have a change of clothes – and then the years of Warren and Harry Dean each dressing you up in variations of baby dolls, The Money meant even something so little as buying your own clothes.

You could look classy.

But, still, neither you nor Paul ever said a word about The Money.

You knew to always choose the most lavish option.

You'd never be expected to pay anyone back.

It was a privilege to no longer speak about The Money.

Sure, in a way you two talked about it all the time as everything you ever said to each other took it for granted.

But you never talked about it specifically.

Would've been bad form maybe for either of you to ever admit that it had not just always been that way.

You had never even been on an airplane before meeting Paul.

When would you have been?

Running away from Long Island to Manhattan at sixteen or running away from Manhattan at seventeen?

No.

No way.

With Harry Dean?

You had never been on an airplane before and now you played along each day, Yes, everything perfect.

Paul was not oppressed by perfectionism like Warren.

He didn't need to be.

For him, everything was OK.

*

And those two made it obvious in every possible iteration and flutter, Paul and Diane *had* met somewhere before and were re-establishing their mutual crush.

Their flirting codes had been established well before the party, and that afternoon the codes would only deepen in sophistication.

And Diane, even though she was there with her boyfriend, she apparently had no sense to know to keep her cool.

She gawked and blushed with Paul like some bobby-socked Midwestern teenager from his fan club.

And worse, he *liked* it.

You'd watched Dennis and James drag race in The 55.

You enjoyed it some, watched it for your own sake.

Warren didn't care if you watched his cockfights and that meant that you enjoyed the ones you did watch.

Then of course Harry Dean expected you to be his cheerleader as well as his photographer.

But Paul, the scale he lived publicly, you couldn't watch him perform if you wanted to.

You could only watch the people watching him.

So funny, compared to Harry Dean and his sense of being looked at everywhere, insisting all the time that you photographed everything like his personal still photographer.

So what were you to Paul, a groupie?

Was that what models retired young to do?

You weren't ambitious.

You weren't a fucking artist or a poet or a philosopher or a goddamn revolutionary.

And you didn't want to have to pretend to be for anybody.

You left the dumb world of New York *Blowup* for the flimsily constructed motel furniture of America.

And Paul's Christmas Party, this was how he celebrated Christmas, how warped the fears of a middle aged man can get when that scared little withering man has been looked at too closely for too long?

He needed four hundred guests for his groovy, jazz-flute Christmas, a valet at the end of the long driveway, backless dresses.

187

*

Dancing a half-time cha-cha together, Paul told Diane – *You could stay here. We could make the whole record in six weeks.*

The chandelier on the porch was bigger than any other porch you'd ever seen.

From your home in the trees on a hillside, Beverly Hills architecture was visible in the distance, just barely: French next to Spanish next to Japanese.

Perfectly placed curling glass sculptures were woven through your metal shelving.

Precisely because gamecocks are the stupidest creatures, they are also the most intelligent fighters.

But they're so stupid, sometimes one bird just wanders out of the ring and that ends the match.

You would have liked to tell Paul about that.

You liked the cactus on a pedestal in the crowded room; it made it different.

And you bet people thought you'd put that there special for Christmas, but no.

And you had that white Christmas tree, because even though trees are green and everyone knows trees are green, snow is white and there was no snow to be found in LA.

Not even Paul could round up that.

And really, in the glare of all that glass and the green sunlight beyond, should Diane Keaton in her stupid men's suits really have somehow been a threat to you?

*

After dark, angular shadows thrown by decorative lights transformed the house.

The party's volume thickened.

You hid in the loud crowd and watched Paul and Diane, shameless on the dance floor.

A graying mustached man pressed in tight against you and made bursts of conversation while he danced, his sour breath hot on your cheek.

You shouted over the music, each syllable enunciated – *My father died when I was still a little girl; he misdiagnosed himself, thought his leukemia was lung cancer.*

The room swelled and released around you and you focused on a floral arrangement, its pedals spinning outward from its center.

All color had been sucked from the room.

Paul held Diane's fingertips lightly, dancing a little cha-cha again, redundant to even watch.

Not that you wanted to dance with him ...

You watched a beautiful young girl with big eyes dance on her own.

She smiled effortlessly at the men who approached her, but never responded a word to any one of them.

Another man pressed up against you and you talked while you danced. – *I used to know all the constellations, and I could name them all and point them all out. When I was younger.*

Diane submitted to Paul's dry hump on the dance floor and Woody Allen was nowhere around to intervene.

You approached the floral arrangement and fingered a petal lightly, soft hairs on supple flesh.

It smelled like an aerosol spray.

You watched that young girl – big pretty eyes – sway alone.

Dancing pressed up to a different man, you told him – *I don't know. Now it's all a big mess. I look up at the night sky. I can't tell what's what.*

Slow and concentrating, you methodically dismantled the floral arrangement, plucking clean anything that jutted from the end of a stem, carefully tearing each leaf in half one at a time, one at a time.

The bouquet included one big feather and a smattering of seashells.

The torn flowers all dropped into a pile at your feet, you fanned them out into a swirl on the tiles with your toes.

Some gunked up and got smashed up with the cracked seashells.

Still dancing, bouncing in place, hot-eyed and smiling, people stepped back to stay out of your way.

You cracked the feather.

*

Your friend the other model, so particular about her makeup; you struggled to comprehend such a bad idea executed so carefully.

In a booth late one night with two guys, a couple years older, both had conservative fades and nice clean shoes.

One, nostrils flared, completed his straight-off-the-Mayflower style with a tweed coat over a sweater vest.

The other, with his high WASP-cheekbones, awkwardly wore beads over a dashiki.

The bar's walls were husky stained-wood, knicked with splintering divots, a long mirror behind the bar.

Hard-bop played.

They all nursed small beers while you finished a cheeseburger and goopy milkshake, double-order of fries.

The guys' conversation felt like a performance for the sake of you and your friend.

That's not the way to run a class.

You're too hard on the old guy.

But the syllabus – even the syllabus –

Yeah, I know, but –

But nothing, it's all designed wrong. Fundamentally. It's just the wrong approach.

Fitting the sloppy last bite of your cheeseburger in your mouth, you crumpled your napkin and pushed aside your plate.

The waitress returned and the other three all ordered beers.

The pulsing hard-bop paused.

A faint knocking rang through the vents.

The reflection of the one guy's back got cut off at a strange spot in the mirror behind the bar, doubled perpendicularly, his beaded necklace and the stitching of his dashiki fanned out into a doily.

You ordered a whiskey.

The guys looked surprised, but your friend the other model, liked the idea and ordered a whiskey too, please.

Two whiskeys and two beers. – The waitress said and walked off.

You all sat quiet, taking turns sighing, looking over and beyond each other to survey the room.

You watched the room's backwards motion in the mirror behind the bar.

The Mayflower guy, his tone awkward with sudden excitement, said his father told him to invite some friends out next weekend before they have to dock the boat for the season.

And even the invitation felt like more performance.

The waitress arrived and set down the drinks, ladies first. – *Whiskey, whiskey, beer and beer.*

You lifted the whiskey to your lips and threw your head back, downed it in one gulp.

You shivered, happy to feel its warmth run down your throat, down your spine and back up again into your head.

Pulling your coat up over your shoulders, un-bunching a tangle from one armpit, you stood.

Let's go. – You pulled your friend hard by the wrist, bumping her against the table.

Explained you forgot about this thing.

The guy in the dashiki asked if it was something they said.

Your friend the other model, stood and smiled nervously to your dates, pulled her coat and purse up against her chest in a bundle.

She downed her whiskey in one gulp and shuddered.

You dragged her across the floor dense with tables towards the door.

Gaining her equilibrium, she bounced the last few steps.

With sarcastic waves, the young men left sitting confused called out across the restaurant. – *Really nice, girls. Real classy. We'll be calling you.*

*

Out into the Manhattan streets, the night thick with twisting glows from every depth and height, you and your friend the other model spun around the first corner you came to.

Teetering on falling forward, the momentum of your steps hard to keep up with, you both laughed, your friend the other model, more than you and more nervously too.

Breathing deep, you walked, pulling your friend behind you with purpose.

– *Come on.*

I'm coming. Where are we going?

Come on.

Where are we going? – She anchored her feet hard to the sidewalk and leaned over, hands on her knees to catch her breath.

You stopped, annoyed after a couple more steps, and returned to her, grabbed her by the arm. – *Come on.*

You're crazy. Where are we going?

I don't know.

Then what's the hurry? – She asked and you shrugged.

Gasping, your friend stood up straight, dropping her shoulders back exactly as the modeling coach instructed you to do for proper posture.

Her makeup looked so ridiculous to you.

You surveyed the street: endless shades of slick purples and browns, not a straight angle anywhere.

Other side of the street: a hip cowboy, done-up perfectly to the highest standards of machismo-vanity came strutting in your direction.

You grabbed your friend by the arm.

You trotted across the street, took a few long steps to catch up to the hip cowboy as he passed.

You called out – *Hey!*

And he stopped and he turned and he smiled big and naturally and bright when he realized you were addressing him.

But by no means did he appear surprised.

*

You closed your door on the Christmas party, pulled the beautiful young girl along with you, the one with the big eyes that you'd been watching on the dance floor.

Stepping out of your giant walk-in closet with your arms full of clothes, soft and thick, you tumbled them all on the bed next to the girl.

The girl smiled up at you, that same smile you had seen her give the men that approached her as she danced.

I don't understand why you're doing this. – The girl said and you had no idea how to explain.

Excited, you thought you'd like to tell her about how you used to be saving up for a private island, and the coyote you kept as a pet in New York City.

She was beautiful, sublime freshness and health, so taut.

You scooped a couple Valium from the dresser ledge, extended your palm to the girl.

The girl shook her head no.

You swallowed them both dry, one at a time.

You weren't sure what you were doing and why.

When someone becomes aware of being gentle, the desire to be gentle, was it because gentleness had ended as an intuition and now required specific effort?

Or was that awareness the beginning of true gentleness?

It would all be so simple if you could only explain to the girl.

– These people, they all grow up and get sober and talk constantly all the time about how they used to self-medicate, but now they've really got everything all together and how they've never been happier ...

The girl looked at you.

You were failing to explain, but the girl was beautiful, content patience and pliable will.

You leaned low and put your palm flat against the girl's cheek.

You wanted to look at her deeply, but struggled a moment to see her through the blur.

She just sat, didn't shake or look away.

You're beautiful – You told her and the girl stood up,

turned a small circle in a few steps.

How old are you? – You asked. – *Seventeen? Eighteen? Seventeen.*

You picked a light dress up from the bed and held it up to her. – *I knew it. These will all fit you perfectly.*

I told you, I don't need your dresses.

You knew that you had indeed heard the girl.

But for some reason, you didn't know why, but it was like you hadn't.

You sat down on the bed.

Seventeen. – You said with a sigh.

The girl smiled at you, and you recognized the condescending effort that she put into it.

You shook your head.

You had to explain.

– All those people …

You waved to the bustle beyond the bedroom door.

– Their best work is behind them because they used to live fearlessly, whatever it took to be able to do that. So what, you know? They lived fearlessly and so they were able to create things, beautiful things for example, or even not create things but just live fearlessly, and that was beautiful too. But now they talk all day about how they've never been happier now that they're cleaned up and got everything together, they have mortgages …

The girl moved towards the door. – *I really should go find my friend.*

Jumping up, you pushed an armful of sweaters and dresses at her.

Wait. – You said, surprised by the volume of your own voice.

– Take all of them. And I have sweaters and blouses.

You stepped back towards the closet.

I don't want any of it – the girl told you.

But I have dozens and dozens of –

I don't care.

Well then, sell them. Keep the money.

I don't need the money.

194

You just wanted to explain, you needed to, it was simple and you didn't know why the girl was fighting you about this.

The girl didn't know everything that you knew about men, about taking care of yourself, about keeping your head and getting by.

How could she?

Seventeen.

You touched her elbow softly, needed to slow things down.

You weren't sure how or what to ask her exactly.

But you, who were you to teach anyone anything?

You'd never learned how to be alone.

That's one thing you need to figure out on your own, no one can teach you or tell you how.

But ... – You said, looking at your toes and then back up at the girl.

– ... Who will take care of you?

The girl pulled away and started towards the door.

But you're really going to need these, you know. – You said.

But how could the girl have known?

The men all get so self-important and you won't want to have to ...

The young girl smiled, her eyes so big and kind, smiling at you as she closed the bedroom door behind herself.

You sat down heavy on the bed.

*

PART 4

Bad Timing

(1979)

I remember you sitting on the bed.

The big brass bed looked southwest down into Central Park.

We'd both been up all night.

You left me.

You left me your journals and photos and the memories.

And I became immersed, far more interested in them than in getting on with the day-to-day of citizenry or whatever.

And I accepted that I'll never get over it.

You left me.

The pink of your blush; I've lived a life of *devotion to beauty*.

We both wore white cotton t-shirts from Redfish Lake in Idaho.

We both had them before we met.

At night you wore only that.

You were my mirror, I know, and you were flattering.

You loved pears enough, you'd spoon pear juice from tins.

I should've known.

When the bird brooch broke I should've known.

Its beak cracked.

Sadness fits my part.

Shooting continued.

Two in the afternoon, I threw a ten-foot shadow on the promenade above the East River Drive.

And the birds flew free in the streets of New York City.

*

I only wanted to make my way past you, but you threw your leg up against the wall, blocking my passage.

It was you.

You were the assertive one at that party when we met.

You said – *We're going to meet anyways. May as well be now.*

I told you – *If we don't meet, there's always the possibility that it could've been perfect.*

You warned me that the roads were wet, and I promised you that I'd drive carefully.

You gave me your number on a book of matches.

I was practically begging you to let me down the hall, sweating in my tuxedo with my giant bowtie.

Finally I bent low to crawl under your leg.

*

You wore lots of blue when we first met, and purples.

Any time that you weren't done up perfectly, you were a mess, like there was little day-to-day upkeep.

You usually let shaving and showers go until you got really done up.

First couple times we saw each other, you were like a different person each time.

I could never know what you were thinking.

I never knew what to expect.

Your hair would be different every time, sometimes straight and sometimes in loose curls.

One afternoon we had no plans, but you wore an elegant blue evening gown.

And you were only interested in sex when someone was waiting in the other room, or at the expense of getting some afternoon obligation done.

You bled money.

I could never guess where your money was coming from.

Occasionally you'd make a comment about a decision being made according to money, but I never witnessed it.

You'd talk about never owing anyone anything.

But mostly it was clear, immediately, that whatever access you might ever grant me, it would never be to your thoughts.

Your interior life was all your own.

We'd talk about art.

You were always so thrilled to talk about art: painting, poetry, music, fashion.

You were never self-conscious, always looking around side-to-side or past me.

I was always watching you in profile.

I knew the sex at strange times thing, it was because you were so happy just falling asleep with me every night.

You wanted to keep them separate, sex and sleep.

I got that.

But still, you just drove me so crazy.

It was like a compulsion.

It was like I really couldn't keep my hands off of you.

I couldn't help but try to climb on you, even though I knew that you didn't appreciate always being pressed for sex.

*

You sat on the bed.

We'd both been up all night.

In the mornings, unimpeded by any taller building's shadow, light drenched our penthouse, every surface: thick fabrics brightened and dark woods reflected, paintings revealed the depths of their brushstrokes.

And if you could do anything, if you had acquired any one skill in which you prided yourself, it was going blank.

You figured that's how all the other men before me had always wanted you, so they could just project whatever they wanted upon you.

So you knew that nothing would make them angrier than giving them far too much of exactly what they thought they wanted.

And you knew how good you were at it.

You recognized the limitless agility of your own blankness whenever you witnessed the comparatively stunted attempts other people made: unaccounted-for twitches, irrepressible sneers.

You could go blank like no one else you'd ever met could.

And you knew how to use it.

That morning on our big brass bed, you stared.

You slowed your breath, eyelids lowered into narrow slits to limit the light allowed in, hardly blinking.

You locked your posture.

No expression of yours would give anything away or betray any inner condition.

That was the thing you had, your advantage: unreadability, unreadableness.

*

But the realization had been creeping up on you.

It was like straight out of your beloved *Bell Jar*: "The silence depressed me. It wasn't the silence of silence. It was my own silence."

It may have been abstract, but it was very real.

And you knew it.

And only then, on defense against the glare of the bulbs of our big brass bed, could you no longer ignore it.

You were losing your grip on that one thing you had, your advantage.

We hadn't even known each other long and I could see it.

Sure I may have been a successful Research Psychoanalyst, but I think it would've been clear to anyone.

Your blankness, however practiced, had come to reflect without filter *The* Blankness – True Blankness.

What had always before been only a front had become your true condition.

To someone else, from the outside, your surface remained the same.

But what had always before been affectation, had become True Blankness.

Any sense of potential satisfaction had dimmed – not vanished, but faded.

And apparently it had bundled your restlessness up along with it – no more potential satisfaction, and no more restlessness to even attempt to find satisfaction.

And wherever they had both gone off to together –

Satisfaction and Restlessness – at least their union tempered this loss of potential satisfaction.

Is that hope, relief from hope?

You were left with only True Blankness and its inherent balance.

Better than being restless.

You had ceased to process any value judgments and you were aware of it.

And if your one thing, your advantage – the mask – had truly slipped and your blankness itself then shined, your awareness of its slippage at least provoked some mild new curiosity.

You checked your posture against the dangle of a curling bang tickling your cheek: with your head held at the proper angle, chin lowered just so, you could trust your eyes remained hidden.

This cued you to part your lips, to work the expression to your advantage.

Simple breath, steady, displaying your full lips which, you still knew, you remembered verbatim how they said it, back when you were in New York before – your lips *popped like a small rosebud, resonating with the blush of your cheeks against your skeletal complexion.*

But you weren't trying to be yourself in New York again, were you?

Did going back there create that confusion: the-you-who-you-had-become versus how you knew to be yourself there?

And when your bangs tickled your cheek, you knew to breathe and posture to your advantage, bend right.

*

You weren't looking, wouldn't look at me.

So I don't know why I hollered – *Would you please stop staring at me like some kind of stupid wounded fucking animal!*

And even then you still didn't look.

You hated to give me the satisfaction of flinching.

203

Curling one leg under you, you brought your other leg closer against your chest and pulled your oversized white t-shirt down over your knees.

In the blast of air conditioning, you weren't looking at me at all, let alone staring.

And I couldn't wound you.

I pivoted quick and back and turned again, throwing my entire weight into short lunges while actually remaining in place.

Such was the effect you had come to have on me.

I drew a long drag from my cigarette.

I was thirty-eight years old, fit and in control but I could not stay blank like you.

I bent backwards, stretched my lower back.

My stupid temper.

You always shut down, which made me even angrier, more demonstrative of my anger.

I contorted as if it was necessary to do so, to wrestle out my slow textured moan.

Moving my hands to my hips, I inhaled deeply, low into my abdomen and fixed my eyes on you.

But you wouldn't look back at me.

You wanted me helpless and frustrated.

I hated that you could keep your cool whatever my stupid outburst, and I especially hated that you could keep quiet against however loud I got.

With self-conscious composure, I put out my cigarette.

I spun and with a few steps, walked out the door.

I saw you flip over in the bed and look out over Central Park, a chill on your bare ass, before I closed the door.

You always loved that we sat within the skyline, our window just one more blinking dimple in the grid, flattened against the sky.

All the people on the street below each so tiny from above, you sure didn't feel flattened against the sky.

Flatten*ing*, being pressed, maybe – but not flattened.

Time passed.

I never stepped away from the door.

204

You liked to follow one little dot along the sidewalk a couple blocks, then choose another specific dot to follow when you lost track of the first.

You sat that way long enough, you started your game over again and again, taking your time in-between rounds, forgetting that you had just imagined someone you would never meet, and their plans for the day, and how this day fit into each of his or her other days.

While you were squinting, your forehead still pressed against the thick glass, I returned.

I lit another cigarette, stood at the bed, hands on my hips.

My shoulders dropped when you turned back around to look up at me.

I sat down on the bed next to you and hugged you against my side and pushed you over, and you gave in to my collapse.

More than anything I loved to nuzzle my nose into your armpit.

With a deep sigh after a long pause, flopped on you, my dead weight pinning you to the bed, I finally spoke.

– *I just don't know what you expect of me.*

Pushing me until I sat up, you sat up next to me but said nothing.

I hugged you sideways, the angle and my grip both awkward.

I sat up a bit taller and looked at you, and you looked back at me.

I dropped my head and remained quiet a moment before sighing loudly.

You can come with me. – I said.

Despite yourself, you rolled over a little, an acknowledgement of my comment.

For a moment, I know you imagined me as one of the little dots on the street, hurrying through the giant grid with some unshakable sense of purpose.

I mean if you want to, I'd like you to come with me. – I continued.

You shook me off lightly with a small gesture and returned to looking out the window, down over all the tiny people.

*

We both slept for a little while and by noon, sitting on the bed, you pulled on a pair of jeans while singing your scales to yourself.

I couldn't believe that the other men never encouraged your creativity like I did.

And it made sense that you pursued singing, because I could always help you if your technique slackened, especially with the higher registers.

Your vocal coach told you that though your deep speaking voice came fully from your throat, you sang entirely through your nostrils.

Singing scales of funny sounds helped to change your breathing.

I brought you a plate and a cup. – *Goat cheese on toast.*

You smiled and faked clapping, but continued singing.

You hated having to stop for any reason before hitting the ends of your scales, getting back to the beginning and the lowest note.

And tea with milk. – I said, placing the plate and cup on the bedside table before sitting next to you on the bed.

Almost done. – You said in a quick gasp between notes.

You're sounding good.

You made a silly face, scrunching your nose while singing.

Smoking, I watched you, my stare intent, my smile small and casual, but held with purpose.

I knew that no one had ever understood you like I did.

*

I should just explain this simply.

I can't be afraid of how it might sound.

Traveling so much, I learned to rely on my smile.

And that taught me all about this.

The power of my sexual energy was its matter-of-factness.

I was attractive, attractive enough that before meeting me,

people would be aware of me as An Attractive Person.

I kept in shape.

And my confidence was that of a person who never had to wonder if he was An Attractive Person.

This in itself didn't interest you, though I know that it did make our sex hot.

For years I know you thought that all you wanted of sex, anymore, was just to get through with it.

Warren was gruff, Harry Dean and Paul both too tender.

But our sex was hot because we kept it so simple – not simple like lacking in daring, but we had a cool matter-of-factness.

We stated our desires directly and without any whiff of shame or bashfulness, and these acts, articulated simply, then began exactly as stated without any warm-up, but also without any aggressive shock – just execution of a task.

Body parts would be presented – *Here it is* – without shyness or reservation, no pride or shame.

And with the foundation of our simple acts confidently established at this higher point, this baseline raised, the acts progressed to climaxes at least that much higher, if not more.

Which was to say: jumping into things by no means meant skipping foreplay.

We'd linger together in any of many simple variations, never thinking of any small act as a means to some ends.

You never thought of yourself as attractive, but knew that the attention men gave you was not common.

And you were never self-conscious.

Is feeling beautiful actually just that simple for a woman, not feeling self-conscious?

The true gravity, the difference such confidence gave An Attractive Person which made sex better with An Attractive Person, was the lack of any kind of self-conscious attempts at dynamics.

For us two, simple repetition intensified itself.

I had the confidence to know to wait for it to intensify itself instead of pushing it forward toward some false premeditated idea of a peak, which in fact would never reach as high as the true peak you could reach if you submitted to the act's own power instead of attempting to propel it.

It would seem this could be an acquired talent, but you didn't think so.

You thought it was more simply the grace granted to Attractive People, a birthright.

Who but An Attractive Person could have the cool collectedness to simulate the act more than aim to lose oneself in it, and in the simulation get consumed?

*

And I know it's true, so I can just say it.

The funny thing about me was that people, our friends in common, always used the same word to describe me: smart.

But I was not that smart.

I was by no means the dumbest man you'd ever been with.

Dennis, if you were to count him on his own – which, you didn't think of you two as having ever really been together as much as you kind of had the thing with him *and* James – but even in combination, even with the bump in smarts James offered them as a duo, they still must've been the dumbest.

It was a rude standard to rate exes.

But what standard wasn't?

Harry Dean, much as you did love him simply and completely, even submitting to his corny taste, he wasn't as smart as me.

And that was the point of this rating system – to put my smarts in context.

So you could admit it.

It was rude, but true.

You never thought that I was as smart as you.

Paul probably wasn't as smart as you either, but I know you thought he was smarter than me.

Of course in your mind no one would ever be as smart as poor, suffering, self-sabotaging Warren; the efficiency of his mute expression, the vast dimensions of his imagination in making connections.

But there was a meaningful difference between all of them and me.

You never had to consider the smarts of any previous lover so much.

You were compatible in your ways, savoring negotiations, enjoying each other as you did.

And it wasn't that I was the most self-centered man you'd ever been with.

Brilliant, unable-to-take-care-of-himself Warren obviously had that covered too.

But you had never known anyone that identified so completely with an idea of himself that you so disagreed with.

Everyone else believed like I did.

Our friends in common believed it.

Everyone told you – *Oh, Art. He's real smart.*

That's what everyone said, without exception.

But even I knew the truth.

And you were the only one to ever see through it.

People just thought I was smart because of the confidence with which I'd speak.

I never asked any questions, never left any room for differing opinions or even shading in my statements.

I had always been an answerer of questions, with confidence – *This is how it is.*

But that confidence which everyone mistook for smarts was nothing more than the confidence of being An Attractive Person.

I was never one of those scorching-hot, flashy hard bodies.

Those poor souls – blessed as The Attractive People were to a lifetime of sexual satisfaction that the less fortunate could never even comprehend – that miniscule sliver of Perfect-Looking People; that was different.

The Perfect-Looking People were not attractive.

Everyone knew that.

They were grotesque, cartoonish perversions of the human form suitable only to the hormone-drenched pubescent and the suburban.

Those freaks were doomed to be stared at as *Other* and never know human-connection.

But the Attractive People, we got away with things – for example, people misunderstanding my confident declarations as brains – because people didn't recognize The Attractive People as attractive on a conscious-level.

No one ever thought they were *unattractive*.

And sometimes one might fall into a stunned stare, in certain lighting on a particularly overcast afternoon, or wet hair falling just right.

But set next to The Perfect People, those monsters that people thought of as attractive, The Attractive People seemed like, well, just perfect.

Perfect enough to make people say *smart* when they just meant attractive.

*

Bouncing on your toes, you stood a step behind me at the bookstore while I bought it.

Together we strutted quickly back to the car, my shoulders swinging and lips pursed.

I teased you, not letting on that I was in a hurry.

And you got silly and wild you were so excited.

You kept pulling at my sleeve, and we both trotted.

You grabbed the bag from my hand and then we were running together, darting side to side through the crowded foot traffic on the sidewalk.

Leaning on my low car, its roof hot in the afternoon sun, no shade anywhere in the city, you tore open the bag.

Struggling to balance the book, you had to dig a second, took both hands to fold the bag inside out to find the cards.

I snatched the book from you.

You spread the colored cards out on the roof of the car, but I told you that orange isn't a neutral color field so it wouldn't work.

Careless in your excitement, you scooped up the cards and with a thump, dropping your elbows heavy, fanned the cards out on the roof of the white sedan parked next to us.

When I first told you about this, your initial thought and you said it, was – *That is so stupid.*

Sure, it was my field of expertise and I was well respected in it, but that on its own didn't convince you.

Only when you insisted there was no possible reason that it should work and I explained quite well why it did, did you get excited.

Sensory perception of color is objective. – I looked at you. – *Right?*

You nodded. Maybe, OK ...

Well, color preferences are subjective. – I stared at you.

You shrugged and nodded again – *sure.*

This distinction allows subjective states to be objectively measured by using test colors.

You groaned, didn't want to, but couldn't help it.

You spun away from me.

Patiently, I explained to you how the cards revealed the individual neither as he perceived himself nor as he would like to be perceived.

I explained the twenty-three personality traits, many of which – I adopted a playful Vincent Price impression – *lie outside the realm of consciousness.*

And by the time I finished explaining it, you insisted that we run to the store immediately and try it out.

The cards spread out on the white car, I instructed you to line them up.

– *Your favorite color, the one you're most sympathetic to, then your second favorite.*

Your front pressed to the car's window, you scooted the cards into position.

Slow down. – I said.

I already know which ones I want.

Don't associate them with anything.

You lined them up quickly, bounced up and down on your toes again, felt the pull way up in your shoulders. – *Tell me what it means. I want to know, right now.*

Hang on. – I said. – *Hang on. Slow down.*

Holding the book open in one hand, I flipped the cards over with my other, tricky as they slid against the car.

There were numbers on the back of each card, which the book decoded.

You bugged me to hurry up and looking at you askew, I was playfully teasing you, that I now knew something about you that you didn't know yourself.

I shook my head and sighed before looking at you seriously.

– I don't think you should spend too much time alone.

*

Was the lighting of clubs a conspiracy?

Why should every night out be remembered as red?

You and your friend the other model did go with that cocky hip cowboy-stud that night, when you lived in Manhattan the first time, after you ditched the squares Mayflower and Dashiki.

The cowboy-stud led you to a loud and cramped little bar.

Everything was red.

He winked to the doorman and you were all waved right in, never asked to pull out your fake IDs.

Dark enough, everything that didn't glow red was just a shadow of itself.

Crowded enough, so loud that your voice would carry no further than the ear you leaned into.

Everyone, all those people you'd never seen before but fell right in with, everyone all drinking a lot, fast, and laughing a lot, they all combined, everyone present, into a unified heaving mass.

With a light touch to your elbow and a whisper, as if somehow his right or responsibility to do so, the cowboy-stud severed you from the group, placed you in the care of some short guy, substantially browed and sweaty.

This ratty guy you ignored, tilted away from over and over.

The cowboy-stud leaned in, talking close into your friend's ear, his smile sustaining its widest expanse.

Red everything, dense with bumping phantoms, over and over this little guy returned.

*

You were the one that first used the word, referred to your own *pussy*.

I never would've started using the word, at least not openly and not to you.

It felt freeing to say it – *pussy* – at least for me.

Even if eventually it seemed to be all that either of us talked about, it still felt liberating.

We made love in my office in the afternoon, Freud looking down from up above.

One bright afternoon at a city park, I asked you to move in with me after I apologized for being so nosy.

You grabbed your big purse from my convertible and walked off, said you'd catch a bus.

You gave me a kiss.

And I found your lit cigarette – dropped carelessly or aggressively I couldn't say – burning a hole in my front seat.

*

My brother died in an auto accident. – You said.

– With he and mother gone we weren't much of a family anymore, just ...

You sighed – *People on our own.*

You didn't know that stuffed between the pages of a book I'd found a picture of you piggybacking on a young man, laughing together, a beautiful day by the lake.

Your purple robe was open.

I was listening.

Your walls were crowded with feathered masks and plaster busts.

I always tried to straighten the crooked paintings, but they'd tilt right back into position as if they'd been weighted.

Ever been married? – I asked.

Nope. – You said. – *I hate these sheets.*

*

I'm moving in with you. – You said, as if you were doing me some favor.

Just do one thing for me. Never force yourself to be different from who you are.

Well who am I then, huh? You tell me how I am.

You're just fine if you forget someone is waiting.

Look can't we just forget all that?

What? Forget that because you got on something pretty it changes who you are?

*

You cried and I was always the one that ended up calling after you, apologizing.

When we first saw that Klimt painting *The Kiss* at the museum, you said – *They're happy.*

I know it was a bad joke for a research psychoanalyst to make, but I said – *That's because they don't know each other well enough yet.*

You asked me to take you to my favorite place in New York.

At that moment, looking over my shoulder, a cop was ticketing my car.

I considered these to be equals: the dread of empty buildings side by side, and the dread of buildings set far apart from each other.

And I'd have to walk around with goddamn Chet Baker songs in my head all the time.

I fall in love too easily. I fall in love too fast.

*

We browsed one of your favorite boutiques.

It was sparsely arranged, only a few racks on the floor and only a couple articles of clothing on each rack.

We were both friendly with Tommy who worked there.

And I chatted with him while you ran a finger along the clothes.

I knew that you wanted to fuck him and you didn't care

214

that I could see it.

His long lashes and obvious ambition, it irritated me that he didn't bother to hide the charge between you two for my sake.

Even if I might understand conceptually that it was only natural, the compulsion to want to make your milky skin blush, I would never have the nerve of that kid to not have the manners to hide it.

You knew how it killed me, just the thought of you with anyone else ...

Nervous with small talk, his thug accent popped out a little.

You moved slalom through the racks in a wide-stepped playful soldier march, kicking your legs out straight without bending your knees.

You stopped at a sweater and looked at the price tag.

You knew how it mortified me when you did that.

Planting your feet, you dangled the price tag in your hand, silently, as if doing math.

I finally must've looked so embarrassed that Tommy looked embarrassed for me.

I believe it's $300. – He said, attempting to puncture the awkwardness.

You smiled feigned bashfulness, looked to me.

Get it if you like it. – I said.

It's cute. – You said and moved along to the next rack, back at the beginning for a second pass through the store.

That's when Carly, coming out of the dressing room without looking, just bumped hard into you from behind.

And you didn't see her either.

Her elbow was so hard against your ribs, you banged against a rack and rattled it a little.

Twirling clumsy, she wore a blouse that hung long past her waist.

Carly. – I called out, excited.

You'd never met her before, but of course you recognized Carly Simon immediately.

You often sang me her song "You're So Vain," thought it

was funny.

And we'd talked about its smart, self-referential meta-fiction.

Shocked and off-balance, Carly grabbed you by the wrist.

My god. – She said.

Carly, I didn't know anyone ... I didn't know you were in here. – I said.

Seeing me, the shock softened on her face.

She smirked and nodded. – *Mr. Garfunkel.*

She did a half-spin at the waist to show off the blouse.

I guess I'm excited just trying this on. – She said.

Wonderful. – Tommy said. – *That looks great.*

Really? – Carly raised an eyebrow to me.

Oh yeah. Great. – I said.

You grabbed Carly's hand on your wrist.

Surprised, her face close to yours, she looked at you.

Carly – I continued – *I don't think you've ever met my fiancé, Laurie.*

She offered you her hand and that big, toothy smile of hers.

Hi. – She said.

Carly Simon, Laurie Bird – Laurie Bird, Carly Simon. – I said, knowing how much you hated it when I introduced people by their full names, expecting everyone to have heard of everyone else.

You smiled and nodded.

And how's James? – I asked and the words were out of my mouth before it hit me about your own history with Carly's husband.

You didn't flinch.

But your eyes were cinched, and I could see your mind moving.

Oh he's fine, great. – She said – *Fine.*

You told Carly – *I don't think you want that.*

I nudged you aside.

Yeah, we haven't set a date yet. – I said. – *For the wedding, I mean.*

Yeah, Art. I'd heard. That's great news. Congratulations. Yeah. We're very excited.

216

Really. – You said to Carly, again. – *I don't think you've got the build for that kind of cut.*

I'm glad to hear that James is doing well. – I said. – *You know Laurie and James go way back.*

With an guffaw, Carly set her weight back on her heels and cocked her hip.

That falls funny on your shoulders. – You said.

What are you talking about? – Tommy jumped in. – *Look at that. It's beautiful.*

No. It's a nice blouse. – You stated flatly, and firm. – *But it's not for her.*

Laurie, honey? – I touched your elbow.

Carly looked herself over in the mirror, pulled at the shoulders to see how the blouse would fall back into place.

You know, I've still never met James. – I said.

And you just came right out and asked her the one thing that everyone knows you are not supposed to ask her.

– *So that song is about Warren Beatty, right?*

*

Ringo Starr, late night at his favorite Moroccan restaurant, never left the smallest crack in conversation open for anyone to say *Well, it's getting late.*

He held court and held it tightly.

I always made creative excuses to turn down four of Ringo's invitations in a row before finally agreeing to one.

But however much I dreaded the date in the days leading up to it, once we arrived and it was happening, Ringo always promptly swept me up into his momentum.

Dishes were served at irregular intervals, more orders placed any time a dish arrived, flatbreads and pickles, the standing order to refill anyone's drink as soon as it got below half.

Everyone shouted over each other, hardly able to keep up with the urgency of their own next statements.

You diluted a yogurt sprinkled with savory seeds by pouring melted ice over it.

It was after 2 AM at least.

You had to press your knees together under the crowded table to avoid banging into someone else's knees, sat angled on your chair to leave room on either side.

Most of the people there you didn't know, or you couldn't remember if you'd ever met them before or had only just seen them around.

Some didn't look familiar and, expecting to never see each other again, none of you bothered with introductions.

Ringo never did either.

He had invited everyone, all ex-Californians with money, but he never bothered with introductions.

His exuberance was in itself good manners of a sort.

You didn't know if he assumed everyone already knew everyone else.

But all interactions went through him and the cloud hanging thick from chain-smoking, so we all appeared to each other through a moneyed-dream of opulence and perfect taste.

Everyone drank a lot and laughed a lot, passing around a dish to nibble on, smoking while eating, and ashing on empty plates.

We all raised our drinks for a toast I insisted on doing.

But I immediately got stuck. – *To ...*

I considered how to proceed, and everyone hushed in wait.

Old friends! – Ringo shouted, unable to stand the suspense.

To old friends that can afford this meal! – I added.

Everyone laughed.

Me and Ringo always competed for attention.

Everyone started to tilt his or her drink, but Ringo interrupted again. – *No, no, no.* – He called out, raising his palm flat as if directing traffic.

He breathed deeply, closed his eyes in concentration to get the toast just perfect.

But no words came.

He writhed and twisted in jest, crossed his eyes silly.

I waved him off and drank.

Everyone laughed and drank with jubilation.

You rolled your eyes and sipped.

The table's waves of cheer diminished.

Smirking and wistful, everyone ate with their fingers and gulped their drinks, filling their mouths with purpose and looking into the middle distance.

The waiter delivered another couple small dishes.

Ringo seemed winded.

The group quiet, occasional chuckles scampered off between bites.

That's when James walked up to the table and stood before you, staring.

*

You would've expected that in the years since you'd last seen him, James either would've mastered his Rasputin-stare or given up on it.

And maybe it's just that you'd already been inoculated, but it looked like his same old awkward stare, to you.

He had exchanged the distressed denim of his youth for distressed leather and a scarf.

Strange; you hadn't seen him in years, a man you hardly knew, knew only to cross a lot of territory with in just a couple days, but something down deep in your stomach kicked hard.

I could tell.

You'd hardly thought about him, and never without prompting: you'd see a denim-colored car or maybe a lanky man with a hunched gait and stringy hair.

He never would've believed that you'd gone on to develop that whole life with Warren.

And Warren had never admitted it outright, but he sure gave you the impression that he and those two guys, James and Dennis, they never even finished that marathon to DC.

After you split they just all called it, went their separate ways, never even needed to explain why to each other.

James couldn't even know that Warren went mute or took his vow of silence or whatever.

You kind of wanted to tell him all this, but more so, you couldn't understand why he would even approach you.

Couldn't you both have manners enough to just pretend you'd never met?

You didn't *know* each other.

You never had.

It wasn't like if Warren had walked in and you could've gotten everything – *Where've you been, are you working, are you with anyone?*

You still wondered about Warren every day.

And I knew that.

Why him?

You never could say, couldn't quantify.

But you did wonder, every day.

And still, even this guy James, seeing him grounded you in some way.

Not *grounded*, but dropped hard, plopped you down into the continuity of your life.

And whatever adventures, whatever scenes you'd witnessed, whatever roles you'd lived in, a throughline or any sense of continuity had never been anything that you had come to expect or even look for.

But seeing James – you knew the last you'd seen each other Dennis was telling him you'd burn him.

Lifetimes had passed.

You had been entirely different characters in those eight years.

Eight years seemed like a long time, but when you thought about how much had changed and all those different lives you'd lived in that time, eight years hardly seemed long enough.

And still, even with the lifetimes lived since, your immediate impulse if James did insist on acknowledging each other, if he wouldn't allow you two to ignore each other and play dumb, your impulse was to be playful with him.

To sit in his lap and make out with him, right there in the restaurant.

That'd be a sense of continuity, a throughline.

If you idealized the past even by simply just acknowledging each other, then you'd have to idealize the continuity.

You only even made it with him that one time in the car because you felt bad about telling him he bored you.

Even I understood that, and thought I might break that to him if he insisted on hanging around.

Our table, everyone quiet, watched James and he squirmed.

Excuse me. – He finally said.

Everyone at our table looked to each other confused, hoping to catch a glimpse of recognition or understanding in anyone else's eye.

Aware that James stood over you, his stare on you, you returned to eating.

Picking at a flaky spinach pie, you didn't look up.

Got stuck wondering what possible life, what possible future ever could've been an option for Warren?

What new roles could he have fallen into: a mute bounty hunter or a mute card shark – one more of his many subtle variations on mute cowboy?

Sneering, aware that you thought my smile arrogant and trying to temper that, lighting a cigarette, I asked James – *Can we help you?*

James looked to me for a second, then back to you.

You still wouldn't look up.

Ringo leaned over to you. – *You know this guy?*

Lifting my napkin from my lap, I began to stand up, and Ringo grabbed me by the arm.

My knee knocked the table, clacking crowded plates.

You looked up at James.

He looked you in the eye.

Look pal. – I said. – *I don't know what –*

Excuse me. – James said.

Everyone quiet, looked at him.

I looked to you, but your expression wouldn't give away any explanation.

I apologize for interrupting your meal. – James said, stepping away.

Our table, everyone careful not to make eye contact with each other, all returned quietly to their food, making their small plates seem like meals, picking up a used fork or struggling to scoop up couscous with torn bread.

Across the restaurant, James sat back down with a big boisterous group.

Silent, he stared at you.

Whispering, I asked you who he was, who they all were and you blew me off with a simple answer – *Crazy people.*

I dapped my cigarette out in a lentil soup shallow in the bottom of a bowl.

Crazy people? – I said, my voice rising a little, in whispered irritation.

Yes, they do crazy things.

*

Ringo chuckled, but didn't say anything.

The table waited at attention.

I chewed and swallowed, paused thoughtful.

Oh god. – I said.

What? – Ringo asked, excited.

Furrowing my brow and tilting my head to demonstrate my concentration, knowing I needed to state this exactly right, I paused, cleared my throat.

Ringo raised his glass and the entire table followed.

When we didn't have any money – I began, hushed and dramatic – *We ...*

Glasses raised and waiting, a couple people smirked politely.

We ... – I repeated myself for dramatic effect – *... when we didn't have any money ...*

Shaking my head with a sigh, I lowered my glass.

Blank glances and rolled eyes were the response to the aborted toast.

With some shrugs, a couple people clinked glasses.

I grinned self-consciously, cleaned my teeth with my tongue.

I looked at you.

You poked at the plate in front of you in silence.

Ringo threw his arm around you.

I should steal her. – He shouted with a pirate's menacing smirk.

No, no, no, no, no, no, no. She's different, this one. – I said, waving wildly, my jovial spirit resuscitated.

She looks too good. – Ringo said, looking you over, taking your hand in his.

He raised your hand to his lips and you blinked big and fast to approximate cartoon-blushing.

It was love at first sight for me. – I announced to the table.

You looked at me squarely, rolled your eyes.

No it wasn't. – You corrected me.

Yes it was. – I looked around the table. – *How can you tell me how I felt?*

You didn't even remember me first time we met.

What are you talking about?

We met once before we met the first time.

Ringo half-stood, smiling wide, loved the tension.

He erupted in a chuckle. – '*We met once before we met the first time!' I love it!*

You knew how to appear just serious enough for a moment to make me squirm in front of my old friend.

We did. – You insisted.

What are you talking about? – I said, lighting a cigarette. – *You were in LA. You were living with Paul. He was never going to get married again. No one needs* –

Yes, but before that we met – you cut me off.

No, we didn't. – I looked around the table nervously.

Everyone watched me silently.

You spoke slowly, as if demonstrating patience, reminding me – *Yes. I was standing in line for a movie at the Cinema One or the Cinema Two. I was waiting to see something. I don't remember.*

And we met?

You used to go there, didn't you?

I did. Yes.

Ringo laughed loudly, waved his arms, but the rest of the group remained silent this time.

But I don't remember. – I said, confused.

We did. – You insisted. – *You looked me straight in the eyes and then went away.*

You looked at me severely.

I squirmed before straightening my posture, tilting back my nose.

Across the restaurant, James, at his table of wild men with a few younger drunk women, looked away when I caught his eye.

Even Ringo quieted for a moment, before he busted out laughing.

And that moment, exhausted by the suspense, everyone else laughed too.

I smiled, but looked you in the eye seriously.

I always flattered myself that I looked good for my age.

Young.

But put me around other people my own age, give me a few drinks and I feel my face muscles slacken.

And I'm proven wrong every time.

I really must look my age.

Well, which is it? – Ringo gasped between spurts of laughter. – *You did or you didn't meet before you met?*

I stood up, dabbing out my cigarette, shrugged. – *I don't know.*

I looked to you and pleaded mockingly.

You shrugged and smiled.

Nothing I could do.

You always just thought I am such a phony.

Leaning down, I kissed you big and demonstratively and hearing a cheer from across the room, we both glanced over to James's table.

Silent, as his big group howled for our public kiss, James just stared at us.

I looked at him for a moment, shook my head and sighed before kissing you again, holding the kiss longer than a single breath.

This boy ... – Ringo shouted, waving at me.

I stood up straight.

This boy was the boy genius. – Ringo said.

I shrugged, hung my head as I excused himself. – *I need to hit the head.*

Good. – Ringo said, taking your hand in his again. – *Then I will tell your beautiful fiancé all about it.*

Don't believe a word he says. – Standing, I pointed at you.

It's all flattering. – Ringo said with exaggerated playful innocence.

Then I especially won't believe it. – You said.

Lighting a cigarette, I shook a playfully stern finger at you, blew you a kiss, and walked off.

I turned around smiling, and shook my head when behind me I heard Ringo shout – *The Adventures of The Boy Genius, Volume One ...*

*

I wobbled across the restaurant.

I looked at James as I approached his party, the Crazy People, and paused, steadying my balance before their table.

James narrowed his eyes but didn't blink, operated some concentrated version of his stare.

I stood up tall and squared my shoulders.

Getting quiet and leaning forward, James's friends all smiled, excited for a confrontation.

But with a big wave, I sighed and stumbled on to the men's room, shaking my head.

Ringo was telling you something about being chased by mobs of screaming teens and jumping in a car, or something.

And you nodded along but couldn't pay attention.

You just kept thinking it was funny you had forgotten, but the thing about James, he was just so boring.

Driving in silence all day, you got it.

But occasionally when you would stop, Dennis would check the gauges and look under the hood and James and you would sit silent, in the dirt or on a fence.

Through long awkward pauses, you would count the fringes on your moccasins or finger your long strings of beads.

The implied-menace of some invisible swarming chorus of cicadas with their overlapping patterns in the heat under the thick brushstrokes of the clouds, their hum replaced the roar of the engine and the whir of the road.

Freaky bugs come out every seven years just to fuck. – James pontificated, babbling.

Insect sex, a patterned orgy just before death, countless miniscule acts in miniscule shells; and you'd half-listen but couldn't even look up at him.

When he was silent all day, you would imagine that he had all these interesting insights but was simply economical with his language.

Then he'd finally say something and you'd have to wonder, just what the hell was he going on about?

Yeah, we got a better life than insects, don't we?

Wow, keen observation.

He'd try hard to philosophize, but it'd only demonstrate more clearly how boring he really was.

All that quiet certainly wasn't his coy manner of hiding hidden depths.

Once you even told him how boring he was.

Sure, you were just The Girl to him then.

What did you know?

Still, once you split, they didn't continue on to DC.

They didn't even entertain the pretense that they would.

They all knew the marathon, all of it, was all posturing only for your sake.

You didn't notice exactly when Ringo, continuing on with the same story, turned away from you to a more engaged audience.

I returned to the table after a long while.

I had splashed cold water on my face and ran my fingers through my big hair.

I knew I must've had the look of a man who had been breathing deep, considering his own face in the mirror.

But actually I had slammed the men's room door on my fingernail.

*

It's just the thought of you with anyone else ...

In bed together, naked, almost dawn and both of us cramped and spinning with throbs of drunkenness, I watched the smoke uncurl from my open mouth.

You turned away from me, pulling the cover up over yourself, between us.

That sad Tom Waits song that you liked ended.

I smiled and the smack of my lips was loud.

Even I recognized the change in my tone of voice.

I did love games when drunk.

For a while, I was not only *confident* that I'd caught you in some inconsistent stories about your family, but I was *happy* about it.

I gloated.

It was proof, however flimsy, that I wasn't crazy.

This game felt like the beginnings of that.

How many for real? – I asked.

And you couldn't believe I'd done it, but I thought it well within my rights: I kept the photo I'd found of you piggybacking on a young man, laughing together, a beautiful day by the lake.

Either that guy was your brother or he wasn't.

I mean, what are we really talking about here? – I asked.

I'm not talking about anything. – You said. – *You are.*

I mean, it can't be that many right?

I don't know, Art. This is stupid. Will you drop it?

I mean, just if you had to guess.

You rolled back over and looked at me. – *Well I don't have to guess.*

I sat up excited. – *Oh OK, so then you know?*

No.

Well if you had to guess.

Why? This is stupid.

Because I'm asking you, because I love you and you love me. Just take a guess.

No. – You wrapped the blanket around yourself and got up and walked to the counter in the kitchen.

When I'd confronted you about that photo I'd stolen, you told me that the young man in the photo by the lake was your dead brother.

I didn't believe you.

You upset a balance of dirty dishes by removing a wine glass out from under a distinct pile.

Struggling, you ushered the tumble and clatter gently into place.

By stepping away, you gave me an excuse to raise my voice a little. – *Like, twenty? Or sixty? four hundred? What?*

You kept a postcard of that Klimt painting, *The Kiss*, tacked up on the cabinet.

Occasionally it stunned you.

I'd find you just staring.

I don't know Art.

Well that's why I'm asking you to guess.

This is so fucking stupid, Art. Leave me alone.

You didn't know much about painting, but *The Kiss* and to a lesser degree, his other paintings done in that similar montage-style, gold leafing and love-themed, they struck you hard in some intuitive place.

Their continuous forms across interrupted surfaces represented to you a kind of perfect synthesis between different historical moments that you recognized as distinct, but never would've otherwise connected.

You could look and look, happy just to wonder how.

I climbed to the front of the bed and sat with my feet dangling.

– *I don't think it's stupid. I think I have the right to know.*

Oh do you?

Yes, I think I do. If the woman I love has fucked dozens of men.

I belched and it burned and I grimaced, like maybe I'd spit up into my mouth a little.

I cleared my throat and focused my squint on you.

Hundreds, maybe. – I said with a shrug.

Jesus Christ Art.

I think it's my right to know.

Sometimes I would tell you about my lectures at the university: "We Are All Spies" and "Illusions."

Just you Art, you're the only one.

You approached me as you spoke. – *I was a virgin when I met you.*

No. Don't mock me. Tell me.

I don't know. – You said.

To think I used to apologize to you for being nosy.

You have no idea how many strange men's cocks you've had in your mouth?

You spun and walked away and, setting a glass down hard, I jumped up to follow you, stomping my feet.

You stopped and turned.

Both still a moment, we stood right up against each other.

You're a sick fuck. – You muttered quietly, in an attempt to quell my tone of voice.

At one point you'd liked me enough that even when trying to distance yourself from me, you framed it as if you were doing so for my sake; you were nervous that I wasn't happy with you.

That's how sensitive you'd been, how aware of not hurting me.

You turned and walked off again.

I raised my voice. – *I am? I'm a sick fuck? I'm not the one who can't count how many men –*

Enough, Art.

No. You couldn't name them?

I asked you to move in with me when I suspected you were seeing other people.

And you told me – *I don't own you. You don't own me.*

And somehow it had gotten to this.

Our apartments came to look like two versions of the same mess.

Then we moved in together.

I pinned you against the window and you turned around, and looked down at the street and the sparse population of people walking hurriedly, each alone and silent at that hour.

With a deep breath, you collected yourself.

My arms pinning you to the windowsill, you spun and looked me directly in the eyes.

Sometimes when I kiss you. – I said – *Your hot little mouth, I can't help but wonder how many strange men's cocks have been in there.*

You didn't flinch.

After our first fight – *or serious talk* – I thought, when you wandered off for a walk afterwards, that you had left your lit cigarette on the seat of my car on purpose.

You had called it a show-off car and said it was silly.

And it makes me sick to my stomach to wonder and to know that you could never even know. You couldn't even name those men.

The chandelier hanging above the bed refracted and repeated us like a kaleidoscope, the two of us together cut from glass.

Always suspicious, listening extra close to any stories about your parents, swearing there were inconsistencies – I remembered this or that and it didn't match.

I didn't even believe it was your dead brother in the photos.

So you weren't much of a family anymore, just people on your own.

I would use that against you.

Smiling tight-lipped, you held me a moment in your stare. *I think I'd probably know most of them if I saw them.*

I lowered my arms from the windowsill, turned and lowered my head and chuckled.

You remained at the window, but relaxed your posture as I stepped away.

My back to you, I sighed. – *You'd know any of them if you saw them.*

You watched me step away.

Your defenses were up severely enough that you must've been aware: my defenses are up.

I am a sick fuck. – I admitted it.

I like the nausea. I don't know. Maybe some wires got crossed. – I said, stifling mania.

I turned to look at you, and you walked back over to the counter and lit a cigarette.

Smoking, you could look at me with composure.

I sat back down on the bed, inspecting my hands.

It turns me on to wonder what you've done with all those men. I can't lie. I like to imagine it.

I told you at the time that I'd come across the photos from the lake – the photos of you piggybacking your dead brother – in the pages of a book.

I thought you understood that I intended to keep the photos.

I fell back in one heavy drop and let my arms fall over my head.

Looking up at the blur of the ceiling as if in deep concentration, I smiled.

I stretched to grab a cigarette from the nightstand, spoke slowly and calm. – *I like to imagine it. What trash you are. Hot trash in a three hundred dollar sweater.*

You didn't know what was wrong with me, why I got like that or how I got to be that way when I got to be like that.

And I felt just the exact same way about you.

Anger and fear pressing against each other held you perfectly still.

I rolled over on to my belly and crawled up to the top of the bed, pulled the blanket over myself, my lit cigarette in the ashtray.

I closed my eyes and smiled to myself. – *You little fucking pig.*

*

One night in bed, casual on purpose, I asked you.

It was my right to know.

And you responded – *Nope. I hate these sheets* – when I asked if you'd ever been married.

231

It was like *row row row your boat* to me, imagining the other men and you.

To whom?

To whom?

... Not important to whom?

... To whom?

To whom?

Not important to whom?

... To whom?

... To whom?

Not important to whom?

I never knew: were you married?

Were you divorced?

You couldn't have still been married?

*

Just like she wrote in your beloved *Bell Jar*: "There is nothing like puking with somebody to make you into old friends."

When you and your friend the other model got back to that hip-cowboy-stud's squalid apartment, an oil lamp painted its crawling shapes across the concrete walls, the three of you smoked from a water pipe.

He threw a couple cubes in a couple plastic cups and made you each a brown cocktail, his plastic cooler on wheels set up like a little bar.

You wrapped yourself up in some kind of skinned-animal blanket on the torn couch and watched your friend dance slowly and out of time with the cowboy.

Kissing slowly while they danced, they each balanced a drink in one hand.

You heard your own low voice saying something about your private island and your pet coyote.

Escaping the blur and joy and noise of the evening, you tilted over to one side and began to drift off.

The ratty little man you'd ignored at the bar sat down next to you and had trouble undoing your zipper, your dead weight falling awkwardly.

*

I said – *I want to explain. It's just that I can't stand to think of you with someone else.*

Standing in the doorway, you sounded exhausted and defeated when you said – *I want to be who I am. I want to get up when I want to get up and eat when I want to eat, drink when I want to drink and fuck when I want to fuck.*

You followed me out into the hall.

I walked fast and didn't turn around.

These things were always on my mind.

One had to be worse than the other: the dread of empty buildings side by side, and the dread of buildings set far apart from each other.

I stood a few steps below you on the stairs.

You tugged your panties aside hard.

You were shouting.

And your pussy was with us on the stairs.

– *Come here. Take it. That's what you want? Do it now!*

*

You had thrown bottles and plants out the window at me down below, glass shattering on the black wet pavement.

The neighbors called the police.

Alone in the penthouse early in the morning, you hadn't slept.

You didn't remember me leaving, but when you realized that you hadn't seen me in a while, you looked around and called my name.

You looked under the table and in the closets.

The weird windows up there swiveled at their centers, opened only halfway, not wide enough for a body to squeeze through.

One at a time, you threw every article of clothing you owned, everything out the window, one at a time.

The breeze caught and blew the lighter things away, carried the heavier pieces down to the street far below.

The rush hour commuters looked up at you, a few even stopping to watch.

*

I became obsessed with control: controlling myself, controlling you, how and when I could allow myself to lose control.

You'd been drinking a lot the past few months.

Longhaired Harvey Keitel, the inspector, said – *Someone rings you and says she's going to kill herself. Now that isn't normal, at least not for normal people. Would you agree?*

I told him – *I spent a good part of my life trying to understand what 'normal' means and I still don't know.*

Longhaired Harvey Keitel, the inspector, asked – *Is your girlfriend a bit mad?*

Mad is not an expression I use.

He had the same framed maze, hung up in his office, that I had in my study.

I held your blue bird brooch in my palm and tapped my finger lightly against its pin.

*

Almost two weeks passed.

My black fingernail had been about to fall off for days, but kept hanging on.

At first you didn't leave the apartment much and if you did, you came home early in the morning and snuck in the back.

How many nights I couldn't say, but I parked across the street from your place, waiting overnight, that one song by The Who always in my head – *Who are you? Who Who Who Who? I really wanna know.*

A couple times I thought maybe you saw me.

After we fell down the stairs backwards while fucking,

landed still fucking – your leg had been up on the railing and then the step was cutting into your back – you destroyed your apartment in a sobbing tantrum.

Afterwards, catching your breath, you were relieved and pleased to find your favorite golden-harpist mirror untouched.

Those hours sitting in my car all night collapsed on each other, just sitting.

My throat clenched from the endless smoking, I watched the streetlights' shades change against the same gradually brightening door.

Migraine and nausea from coffee and exhaustion, it was more like a dream than dreaming, everything remained still except for my mind, the watcher's mind, racing.

Legs cramping, shoulders locked, stomach growling and twisted.

Any shuffle on the street, a squirrel or a cab, a paper bag's drift, staring at the blankness of expectation unfulfilled: the hours collapsed.

And then some days – nights and mornings – and I never saw you come or go.

I wondered if maybe you never got out of the bath at all.

Maybe you just kept your bath ritual going all day for those weeks: your special soaps and candles, leaving the door open to listen to records from the other room.

*

I often read you poetry in bed, me topless in jeans, chain-smoking, and you bottomless, white wine and Billie Holiday.

You always drank as I drove us around town.

There was always Keith Jarrett solo piano music and those Klimt paintings.

I was the first man to ever talk to you about art.

I told you about my lectures. – *Through gratification of curiosity one acquires knowledge.*

I could never understand where your money came from.

How did you even afford your own place?

Paul got with Diane almost immediately after you left him, but however that ended, it would've been strange if your money came from him.

Frustrated once, your eyes smeared and completely spent, you told me – *I don't want any fucking thing of mine, let alone yours.*

*

Harry Dean smiled the whole time when you left him.

His eyes got wet, but tears never got heavy enough to fall.

He never brushed the back of his hand to his eyes.

He smiled; his lips pinched tensely, but never stopped smiling, like he wanted to protect your feelings.

As he stood there while you left him, he continued to protect you, didn't want you to feel bad witnessing him hurt.

Dropping you at The Mason-Dixon line, it was such a given that he could never cross it North.

You were leaving The South and leaving him and you never had to come right out and say that it was him that you were leaving, just The South.

You stood together on a bridge in the rain, saying goodbye.

He put a cigarette in his mouth, the lump in his throat requiring it, and you lit it for him.

Looking you in the eye, he took your wedding rings off – yours first, then his.

He did smile.

He tapped your nose with a light fingertip, asked you to call.

It's not really like going away. – You said.

For you. – He responded.

He touched the pin you wore that he'd given you, turned and returned to the car without looking back, his shoulders hunched in the light rain.

Of course I couldn't know about that tenderness you'd shared, even in splitting up.

*

I called Harry Dean.

The television loud in the background, I got the impression that he was eating a late dinner alone and I immediately regretted calling.

Sitting in hanging smoke, the yellow electric hum of my apartment audacious against the night, I had worked myself up into some panic.

And even after all the studying up on Harry Dean I'd done, I never expected to catch him eating dinner at that hour, alone.

My head hung almost between my knees, I held the phone loosely to my ear.

Well, yes. That's what I said. – I told him, miserable and embarrassed, stumbling to explain to him who I was. – *I was lucky to catch you.*

Were you still married?

That was all I needed to know.

You'd just never give me a straight answer, though you felt somehow that you answered all sorts of questions for me – every day, more and more questions.

Of course to me that just felt like every day, more and more questions, not answers.

But it wasn't difficult to learn all about Harry Dean, even from afar.

He was a public figure in his small way.

And Harry Dean – characteristically so genteel to strangers, but never known for his friendliness to Northerners said to me – *Yeah* – gooey with sarcasm – *lucky to catch me. So, uh, to what do I owe this pleasure? Let me guess …*

I was just wondering –

You haven't seen Laurie? – Harry Dean guessed.

Well Yes. It's been over a week now and –

Harry Dean wouldn't tolerate that crybaby bullshit. – *And you don't know her at all son, do you? Laurie Bird, she does fly away.*

Excuse me? – I pulled at my hair, exactly like you always did when stressed.

And you think she'd be coming back here, to me? – Harry Dean shouted with food in his mouth.

I'm just worried. – I tried to calm him down.

Bullshit, worried. – Harry Dean said.

He thought he was seeing right through me no problem.

It's been ten days. – I said.

When I first found out that you'd been married, that was the first of my rages that you ever witnessed.

And it was the first time in a long time that I felt like I'd really lost control.

It was actually just a guess, but you didn't even ask me what kind of snooping I'd done.

I was most angry that you hadn't told me.

You said – *It's not important.*

And my nostrils flared and my stare a beam, I lost control.

– *To whom?*

To whom?

... *Not important to whom?*

You often mocked cockeyed drama, when someone thinks that they've really burned you and said something devastating, but really you couldn't be less shaken, but they say this thing with such a heightened sense of gravity.

It's embarrassing for everyone, the speaker and their target.

And I knew that's how you were thinking of it when I asked. – *To whom?*

The other men like *row row row your boat*: *to whom to whom to whom to whom.*

Well, hell. – Harry Dean said. – *Ten days, I been waiting a lot longer than that.*

Excuse me? – I never could understand how you had been married to a man almost thirty years older than you.

It disgusted me.

Sometimes I worried that that was the only kind of marriage you could even imagine.

I studied the small poster of that Klimt painting that you'd hung at my place.

Harry Dean broke it down simply for me. – *I been waiting for her to get bored with you, or whoever, wherever she's been. And maybe one of these days she'll wanna settle down –*

She's coming with me to Vienna – I blurted.

I'd done my research on Harry Dean.

I thought the advantage should've been all mine.

I was the one that had the prep time to go over this conversation in my head.

Pardon me? – Harry Dean's voice rose.

I hoped that I had knocked him off balance.

We're leaving next week but I don't know –

You son of a bitch –

I'm sorry I called. I gotta go –

You son of a bitch, calling me –

I'm sorry. This was stupid –

Piss off.

He hung up on me.

*

Both times I thought I wanted a child, but at the last minute changed my mind.

You had had two abortions.

You were never hung up on them.

Done.

You did what you chose.

Harry Dean, the second abortion was his.

He didn't see things quite the same way as you.

He was not pleased when you told him after the fact.

When you first told me about the abortions, about how unhappy the older gentleman was, we were in my car.

This was before you told me that you really thought my car was ostentatious and corny.

For some reason you were laughing when you told me – *He was mad.*

And for some reason, I liked that you were laughing while you told me how angry someone else was.

I pulled over.

Leaning over from the driver's seat, I kissed you.

*

You wore a beret and a ponytail when you told me – *Of course I loved him. I married him. He's what I needed then.*

Harry Dean's goddamn charm posed a very real and constant threat to us.

He could just show up again at any moment and fall right into any situation with such ease, it might take a couple days of stuttering to halt how simply you two would fall right back into place.

Being liked came so easily to Harry Dean, it seemed like it was only as a favor to you that he eventually agreed to spare you his charm.

He could enter any room and give everyone the impression that they'd known him all along.

When he turned on his charm, he could give everyone the sudden impression that the room had always been incomplete in some way that they never could've even recognized, until he showed up to complete it.

So the threat was that he might just show up on your elbow, whenever, any time.

You always imagined it would be while you sat in a group and, everyone looking to each other mid-laugh, there he might appear, laughing along.

And falling right back in together, picking right back up.

Something would seem only a little bit off, flipping on the light and taking off your shoes together later that night, ruminating on the good time with the group, pointing out and carefully articulating which precise small qualities you both liked so much in each of your friends.

You'd pull up close in bed with the warmest of snuggles and dimmest of sexual charges, drift off to sleep grinning together.

And next morning, only after making the coffee and sitting a minute, thoughtfully considering the color of paint on the walls, the situation of the small rooms next to each other, the kitchen visible from the living room in only exactly this manner, would you remember that it was not, in fact, this life that he belonged in.

Stunned, you'd chuckle.

He'd respond with a shrug of entitlement.

He might've lingered for days – days you would've undoubtedly enjoyed every moment of: his camaraderie, the familiar old manners together, your old dresses actually quite cute and comfortable, that mint tea he preferred, how could you have forgotten?

How you'd missed all of it and didn't know.

But still, the necessity of that coming sting, the puncture of finally admitting it was not this life of each other's that you could share.

That life had already happened, passed, been given up on.

You each had only the life after that life left to you.

Potentially embodying continuity was the present's most persistent threat.

You've stood among sparse junky trees along a yellow-dotted roadside, at the top of a height when distance itself has become beautiful, and still could the vacuum and thwack of nun justice ever really be outrun?

You've seen the earth and it is so beautiful.

The deep blues swimming naked summoned could be a shocking reminder: sometimes other people might make you nervous because you just love them so much, you worry you can't ever be good enough for them.

*

In Morocco I asked you to marry me.

Our car broke down in the desert and two local men wrapped in loose robes and scarves against the heat, drove us back to town in their miniature truck.

I had to sit in the back with a goat while they squeezed you between them, their hands on your knee.

By way of answering my proposal, you said – *When I'm with you I'm with you.*

Exasperated, I asked – *What does that mean? You have a husband you don't want.*

My own life. You can be a part of it – the biggest part of it. You are the biggest part of it. I love you.

241

You bit my palm playfully.

*

The glare of snow blinding us in the afternoon sun, we stood at the top of a steep ski slope and looked down.

I was confident and you were clumsy and unsure, but both of us beamed with happiness.

Leaning to push off, I called out to you – *Come on.*

Maybe this wasn't a good idea.

A little late now. – I said, holding myself back best I could from the momentum of my plunge.

Oh God. – You said.

Just follow me, OK?

I took off in a wide turn across the slope.

With a scream low in your chest, you pushed yourself off.

I smiled as you shot past me straight as a torpedo.

*

Your red one-piece monkey baby long johns cinching, you woke up in a chalet on the slopes of Aspen.

I was dressing in front of the fireplace.

You stretched, said – *Hey.*

I turned to you. – *Morning* – Crossed the warm brick room and sat down next to you on the bed, kissed you and you moaned and stretched again.

What time is it? – You asked.

I'm walking to the lobby to get my limo in a minute.

You sat up. – *Why didn't you wake me?*

I was watching you sleep.

It's time?

What did we really have left to say to each other?

You groaned and we pulled up against each other tight.

In each other's arms, then you really woke up.

You sprang alert from fuzz, all at once into the shock of me really leaving, stared off over my shoulder while we embraced.

242

I wish you were coming with me. – I said. – *But I understand.*

You stared, silent, didn't know what to say.

You thought only of pressing your cheek to a baking brick of the fireplace, the flat warmth.

My fingernail had fallen off and a very thin layer was growing in.

It was sensitive, and I was careful to make sure that it didn't get stuck to your long johns.

You had never learned how to be alone.

That was one thing no one had ever taught you.

Usually, you had always felt crowded, like you were hiding.

This was good. – You said.

The trip?

Yeah. Good idea to send you off.

Yeah.

I pulled halfway back from the hug and smiled at you, bumped my nose against yours.

Now don't go making any new friends. – I said.

You rolled your eyes and pushed me away.

I got up and returned to the fire to button my collar, tie my tie.

You looked out over the snow blowing across the open slopes.

You know what I was thinking? – I asked you, my back turned.

Hmmm.

You can come to Vienna to visit me, and we can get married there.

You furrowed your brow. – *My dad would flip.*

I returned to the bed and buried my nose in your armpit.

– Your dad? But'd be great. Just the two of us, none of the bother of everyone else.

I don't think so.

No?

No. I'll see you in a couple months.

Goddamn. Why'd I take the position?

Sarcastically, dramatically, you said – *Illusions*, the name of the program that I'd accepted the position in.

Illusions. – I smirked and shook my head.

It really was a job that only I was right for, lectures like "We Are All Spies."

It's a prestigious position you would've been a fool to pass up. – You said, repeating verbatim that same justification you'd been hearing from me for months, in the same flat tone that you'd been hearing it.

I pulled you into my arms and again you stared blankly over my shoulder, nothing to say, really.

*

Back in Manhattan you stood in a crowd on a corner.

Mid-afternoons, the density of elbows on the sidewalk, the speed of their bony angling from every direction, required some renewed attention.

The elbows had a separate society, independent from the eyes above them.

The stoplight turned and the crowd walked off.

You lifted the back of your foot but remained still, your toe planted in place.

Waddling heavy and fast, close to the curb, the bus approached.

You thought to lift and drop your foot, take a step.

The bus didn't stop, didn't even slow down and the hot blackened breeze of its speed passed close to you – puff – proximity practically an impact of sorts.

You didn't move and the light turned and turned again, the crowd swelling and dissipating around you.

You did not move.

*

You never expected to end up back so close to Long Island.

If it had ever occurred to you that you might eventually stop, you must've imagined it so much further away from the place that you'd first left.

244

Back in Manhattan, but no private island and no pet coyote.

Maybe Dee Dee believed that you really hadn't gotten her message when she was in LA.

Maybe she would've just been happy to hear from you.

But the shame, so you didn't dare try to find her.

You once told me – *I just want to be allowed to give where I can, how I can, to whom I can.*

*

Back at your old modeling coach's desk.

It must've been strange to return years later.

The office still overrun with plants, maybe even more green than before, and she watered and tended to them while you spoke.

– Everyone ... assumes ... they know everything about me ... All the men ... my whole life ... every man I've ever ... met ... has ... wanted to ... own me ... Each one ... comes along ... with ... his version of a trap ... to lure me in.

The modeling coach continued with her plants.

The self-righteousness ... condescending ... to love ... the easy girl ... And everyone I've ever known ... has assumed ... they know everything about me ... All the men ... I was a type ... A girl ... who'll never ... get married ... a girl ... who ... shouldn't ... have children ... And the women ... the women ... are worse ... They all ... know ... my type ... just by ... looking at me.

Tucking her hair behind her ear, the modeling coach peeked back over her shoulder at you but returned quickly to the plants, her shoulders lifting and falling, her head shaking.

Every man ... I've ever met ... has ... wanted ... to control me ... You know ... how ... that looks ... coming at you?

You paused, looked to the modeling coach for a reaction.

Your silence got her to glance up at you.

Didn't she remember how much she always liked you because, like in *The Bell Jar*, when they asked you what you wanted to be you wanted to be everything?

She shrugged, suggesting you continue.

Swooping in all the time ... Hovering ... above you ... and ... hovering around you ... and then ... there's ... the poets and ... romantics and ... self-righteous ... fucks who think ... only they can ... recognize ... my Rare Beauty *... And only ... they ... will ... condescend ... in some Christ-like gesture ... to love ... the ...* Poor Whore *... such self-satisfying bullshit.*

The modeling coach found a manila folder buried between two teeming plants and excited, nodded to herself and tossed it on the desk.

You want ... self-righteous? I'm the one ... crowded ... and ... pushed and pulled and ... I see them ... all ... setting their traps ... and they don't even ... they don't even know ... they're doing it ... and I couldn't be more sick of it ... and yet ... still ... after all these years ... I have ... found it ... in my ... little ... black ... charcoal ... little heart ... to fuck ... every one of them.

The modeling coach paused, raised an eyebrow before returning to the plants. *And what's ... so bad ... about that ... to be greeted with control ... and return affection? ... Who's it ... hurting? ... Who? ... They get ... a trophy to carry around ... They get ... a fuck.*

The modeling coach sat down, set her elbows on her desk with a sigh and looked at you directly, her chin resting on her fingers, folded into one another.

What's so bad about ... two people ... holding each other? – You asked. – *About ... two people ... making each other ... feel good?*

You sat across from each other, glancing, but mostly looking away from each other.

A planter had a leak.

A drip seemed loud.

Tough World, huh? – That's all you meant to say.

Who can choose to deny anyone else some comfort, however fleeting?

That's all you meant.

But it was coming out all wrong and you knew it.

Because that comfort was real, that struggle to suspend

time passing, it actually worked in small bursts.

Promises do *not* get broken.

That's what you meant to say.

Feeling a promise had been broken, that's just part of the feeling itself.

People hold each other only to reject time, reject all that *change* that's so far beyond their control.

The fact that this – the rejection of time passing – inevitably proves impossible does not negate the ritual's execution.

That is the ritual.

Someone will feel betrayed.

That was all you meant to say, but it wasn't coming out.

The modeling coach shook her head and chuckled. – *To be confronted with control and return affection; I like it.*

You sat up straight in your chair a little and reached for a cigarette.

You still look great, and I know it. – She said and you shrugged off the compliment, your lighter flicking.

You're beautiful. You're ravishing. You're stunning. – She dipped her chin, looked you in the eye to emphasize her point.

And – she said – *I have always, honestly, regretted that I was never able to be whatever kind of positive role model you always seemed to need.*

You lit your cigarette.

It's embarrassing for both of us to even have to say this at this point, so forgive me.

You swiped your bangs from your nose.

But you and I have always had a business relationship, never a friendship. – She shrugged.

– And frankly, no one really cares if you're happy and healthy or not.

You nodded.

And? – You asked.

But. – The modeling coach got up and turned back to the plants. – *You're just too old.*

I'm twenty-six.

There's no starting over at this point.

You took a long drag from your cigarette and sighed. – *I know.*

We can't just jump back into things where we left off.

Yep.

She broke her momentum and inspected the leaves of one plant closely, talked quietly to herself. – *Fuck. If this is what I think it is ...*

You got up. – *Well ... thanks.*

I'd love to see you. – The modeling coach blurted, all at once interested in you again.

You should've told her about Bali, the photographer who wouldn't leave us alone.

How when we were swimming naked, you couldn't help but perform.

Yeah, well ... call me ... if you hear of anything.

There are ... – She looked you in the eye – *other ways.*

What?

You're broke?

I mean ... yeah.

*

Late night, you walked around alone.

That Rolling Stones song "Miss You" seemed to play from every open window and every passing car.

A young couple stood in a doorway, the young man pawing the young girl who, laughing, playfully brushed him away.

You watched, curious, not turned-on, but like a third party witness to someone else's erotic dream.

They were your birds and bitches to command.

They were mimes and their groping was a tennis game.

You stood on a corner.

The pointed flashes of city lights blurred and pulsed in your vision.

I see the earth. It is so beautiful. – The cosmonaut said.

A cab pulled up, stopped at the light.

The middle-aged obese cab driver, gray beard and giant owl glasses down at the tip of his nose, looked at you indifferently but focused.

You returned his look, neither of you flinching.

You studied each other closely, each too absorbed in the other to be self-conscious about being inspected.

The light turned green and the cab driver nodded a shallow nod and pulled away.

He could've been your dad or your brother, or Monte or James Earl Jones's brother or Jeff Goldblum.

You might've liked him immediately.

But you didn't, couldn't.

There was nothing of that left in you, whatever that is that occasionally allows one person to feel OK about another person for a second.

*

Nights, it hit you how strange no one to say good night to.

Each day, lacking punctuation, dangled.

Similarly, the mornings, the infinite, miniscule variations of near-identical rituals felt clunky played out without a partner.

However simple it was, grinding coffee or toasting bread, when stripped of collaborative routine down to bare functionality, the tasks lacked punch.

You'd never even noticed this punch before, let alone realized that it was necessary to fully wake up.

This smeared sleep.

It made waking a long slide into the day.

The blanket's return of only your own body heat took adjusting to.

The skin of your torso sweaty under just a t-shirt, while somehow your bare arms still pimpled with chill.

The passing of time expanded and contracted wildly in the dark, as it always had for you.

You'd maybe never slept into a continuous sixth hour, even once since childhood, without pharmaceutical prompting.

It never took you less than nine hours to get a hard-won seven-hour night's sleep.

But without the steady humping snore of some bulk next to you, left without comparative standard or buoy in the steady waves of night-hours, it was like you couldn't balance yourself into the required back-float or scrunch to drift off.

Only Warren, of all the men you'd ever spent a second night sleeping next to, had a similarly manic clash between his waking and sleep-states.

The two of you, both pulling at the twisted blankets, took turns stepping out of the room to smoke and look up at the night, careful to close the door quietly to not wake the other who in actuality only lay in bed awake, sighing for the extra patience now necessary before stepping off for a quiet smoke alone would be a possibility.

The stars were always big and bright when Warren and you were together.

It was a simple byproduct of your drifting, sure, but that didn't make it any less true.

You took more and more pills to sleep through the night until you guessed that you were just staying asleep most of the day, enjoying some long solo slumber party.

Your diet degraded into the habits a thirteen-year-old boy might acquire, if left to his own devices.

But ordering Chow Mein a second time in a single day came to have too steep of a psychic price, too much shame, even if you could justify it in one way as cheaper than shopping.

Frozen pizzas; almost too much effort.

In bed through the afternoons, you would watch the shadows of the greenery that hung outside the window in the wind, dance slowly, projected on the wall across the static shadow of the blinds.

*

Your orb lamp with birds painted on it had always been there and still was.

You had two different statues of The Thinker, one a little bigger than the other.

Home alone, five in the morning, the whole world started raining.

Your bookshelf had always been there and still was.

Your birdcage had always been there and still was.

Your purple robe had always been there and still was.

I was gone.

You were alone.

You accepted it.

You could conceptualize it.

Your white t-shirt showed the stains of hard wear.

No one had ever left you before.

You'd always done the leaving – except for Warren, of course.

But handing you off to Harry Dean so easily, there was never any question of your landing.

You were always a mess except when you were put together perfectly.

You had never been left alone.

But this was not a sexy mess.

Your crooked paintings had always been there and still were.

But now, now you were alone, for the first time not because you chose it– alone.

In theory, yes, me and you were separated only by circumstance, waiting for our marriage.

But you knew how to leave someone.

Better than anyone, you knew.

You were not in a *long-distance relationship*.

You had been left.

Your feather masks and busts had always been there and still were.

And being alone changes everything.

It changes your senses at their nerve endings.

The smallest actions, strung together with silence and without a single witness, ever, they amplify.

You become aware of your self as a form with this mysterious degree of self-determination, always negotiating with your motor functions, a source you've finally quieted your world enough to hear.

Until eventually, the exhausted crash that comes from

attention to this thing that had always been present, just always too quiet to be recognized – that crash.

Your stained-glass mirror had always been there and still was.

In your own living room, five in the morning and storming outside, you dreaded the appearance, wouldn't open your eyes, afraid of your own living room lit differently at dawn.

*

You were wearing only your big t-shirt with a wide stain across its front.

You hadn't left the penthouse in long enough, a couple days at least, maybe a few days, you didn't remember when you would've put that shirt on or taken off your pants.

The warmth of sick days as a kid ...

In neat circles, careful swoops, you cut out your face from all the photos around the house, leaving the shreds of photo paper curling in a small nest on the floor.

And next to that, the small pile of circles, ovals, all flesh-colored: red-eyed, squinting – pained-smiling you.

The newscaster said – *$100,000,000 Sioux Nation land claim.*

The newscaster said – *Pennsylvania State Representative Mark B. Cohen of Philadelphia visited the Three Mile Island site today, on behalf of the Pennsylvania House of Representatives' investigatory committee into the accident there last month. The committee has focused largely on the need to improve evacuation procedures, but after visiting the control room Representative Cohen said it would be 'virtually impossible' for any Control Room operator to keep track of the many variations between the equipment's intended and actual functioning.*

Just sick enough to stay home from school, just drifting without even having to leave, the whole world wonder and music and perfect hurt.

*

The dread of empty buildings side by side and the dread of buildings set far apart terrified me the same.

Hurried, intercontinental long distance costs, you paced while talking to me on the phone.

Afternoon light made the curtains glow.

You asked me – *Well what do you mean, not see each other? I'm already not seeing you.*

I explained best I could and you listened.

You said – *You mean I should no longer look forward to seeing you.*

You were surprised to look up and find the apartment upside down.

You stood on the ceiling, which had become the floor and looked up at the floor, which had become the ceiling.

I'm OK with that. – You said.

*

The energy it took to keep the thoughts out of your head became too exhausting to keep up.

It's like they just kept rushing in, the thoughts flooding you, crowding out any thinking about anything else.

And you tried to keep them all out, but it came to take more strength than you had.

It was that simple.

Like isn't it strange to have once laughed at Warren for saying – *Everything fell apart on me* – and then that same morning to have had sex with James in The 55 in the corn only because you felt bad for having called him a bore?

What happened was simple.

For the first time you started looking back instead of ahead.

You'd always looked straight ahead, zooming, however open the space, however long the party, zooming and never stopping in any one place.

Still seemed true in your feelings or your brain, but now you wouldn't leave the apartment or do anything or move.

And looking back presented you with only more questions, no answers: Me or at least Paul, if not Warren or at least

Harry Dean, or James if not at least Dennis.

You got stuck and this paralysis or disorientation, it feeds itself on itself.

It amasses, like dust and fuzz, like feathers floating ankle high along your floorboards.

And looking back, your behavior all seemed so gross, and the shame.

You had truly believed your own justifications that you later recognized as motivated only by vanity.

Vanity alone inspired your decisions, your positionings – who to leave and when, a hello skipped or exaggerated according to that person's current social ascension or drop.

You remained in position, always in proximity but always distant, so you surprised no one by either clinging or being distant one day to the next – he, then him.

Maybe some primitive impulse guided you; always seeking security, always on the search for some better possible future.

But no.

That'd be just more justification.

Now you had a collection of clippings of yourself from the magazines and papers.

And what good did that do you?

Depression, in a meaningful way, means exactly the inability to express your depression.

Again, it might be primal impulse, some sense of self-preservation – *If I can only continue to express this, if I can articulate the nuances, etc., the grave ambivalences, etc., it could keep me from sinking.*

But wasn't that only vanity too, that fight against sinking?

Everything fell apart on you.

And keeping organized – stacking the mail, which pieces get torn in half and thrown away, which need filing in which folder after reading, which folder goes in which other folder – that became the struggle.

Do not let the apartment get buried in the papers that will be delivered to it, a few each day, too slow of a rate to recognize the buildup from the previous day.

You stood in defense against chaos on behalf of order.

But that confidence it takes to proceed-with-no-confidence, it eats away at you.

And that's how it feeds itself by eating itself – despondency accruing mass.

You accepted it as fact that you were fading, perfectly at ease with the challenge to re-imagine the process, it become a new thing in a new way.

Unbecoming, also a kind of birth once you're ready for it, accepted it and open.

But shame persisted.

You let some of the men take your first name from you; one took your last.

You had let them take your sense of self-determination, years, your ability to express yourself honestly.

It hardly seemed worth it.

You'd learned from all of them, each individually and as a sum.

But the lessons in the end were hardly interesting, let alone meaningful.

You'd given these things away just as much as they were pulled from you.

You'd learned to give everything away, agreeably.

Eventually you didn't see anyone.

Who did you expect to call when you came back to New York?

You weren't going to call my friends.

But you were fine with that.

No one was stranger to you than people you once knew.

And even imagining company, you'd just visualize people lining up to become boring; their proud tone when they told you, coy – *Oh didn't I tell you, me and whoever are getting a place?*

And that tone like it deserved congratulating? – *Oh wow, good job, I always suspected you were unworthy of love, but guess I was mistaken. Turns out that you do have the strength of character to compromise for the sake of conformity. Boy I sure am proud.*

The one thing you learned from all of them, the one thing

that meant anything in the end – you didn't need any one of them.

You never wanted to be anything when you grew up.

And things were changing, fogging, clouding over.

You fought back, leveled the field, introducing your own familiar fog and clouds to greater and greater degrees.

If it was going to be foggy anyways, better off in a familiar fog.

Patiently, you could pass an entire afternoon coiling a braid around your head.

*

You did see your friend the other model one time back in Manhattan.

She stepped out of a cab that you were getting into.

It felt fated.

She was talking to another woman and they each had a child with them and some shopping bags.

They all looked very nice like they had money.

But also, she looked beautiful like she would always be set apart, her grace its own reward.

You wanted to offer to carry a bag for her.

You wouldn't dare pick up a child, but you could at least make yourself useful.

Banished into anonymity when she looked right at you blankly, you almost said something.

*

You were drinking gin, early morning, couldn't have been long until sunrise.

You decided to sit and write a letter, figured you'd know to whom by the time you reached the end.

With a couple knocks of its edges against the table, you enjoyed setting your paper up straight, sitting up straight at the dining room table, pulling out your pen with a brisk wave, a gestural flourish of formal pageantry.

But you fell into a stare.

It'd been just waiting for you.

It was neither your stare itself nor The Open expanding beyond the dense and crumpled party-aftermath of the penthouse: beyond the trees outside, beyond Manhattan, New York, America, but It – *It* was the swirling of the two – your stare and The Open.

It was waiting for you like a hole dug in the forest, covered in brush, waiting for your cursed step.

Your own dumb weight, with no intention to do so, would throw you under, and impale you on sharpened sticks pointing upright, swallowed in the rushing breeze and rustle of the forest floor.

But there had been no party to leave that aftermath, dense and crumpled, fossilizing.

With an assertive, throaty sigh, you did finally lift yourself from the stare.

You hadn't been impaled.

You focused the stare, locking it into place on the white of the page, began to write, mumbling to yourself as you did so.

Aiming for that bottom-right corner, you tumbled in curlicues to the end of the page, and you smiled to yourself big, satisfied when you reached it.

But the satisfaction thickened and the smile warped.

Look, looking close, through the curlicues, your handwriting was an illegible scrawl, un-decodable.

*

1:30 AM: The pills and drinking from the big bottle.

10 PM: The pills and still drinking from a glass.

 I would've looked at the clock.

Your purple robe hung open.

There were moments: you crawled to the bookshelf and on your back, gagging.

But the moments didn't seem connected.

You didn't know how you got from crawling to the bookshelf to gagging, what happened in-between.

How long had you considered the purple of your robe and pulling it closed?

Was that it, nothing more than the purple of your robe between the moments?

The purple of your robe in the party-aftermath ...

After you really took the pills you made a phone call.

I'll be dead. – You told the dial tone.

Dead. – You told the busy signal.

I was a chain smoker.

It was interesting to guess how many beer bottles each with a warm, bitter swallow left at the bottom got kicked around that place.

How many?

You could fill the room with smoke like I would have, move through the smoke in the room like a dream.

Your throat stiffened, moved in from every side toward itself in the slimming middle.

And coughing turned to gagging if you didn't concentrate.

You thought about your heartbeat.

The big bottle lubricated your throat.

You thought about your heartbeat, keep it up.

You read your favorite parts of *The Sheltering Sky*, listened to your favorite African drumming record.

My home was meticulous – black metal, glass, beige curtains, beige seats.

I'd sit in it in my beige coat.

One night I found you *making a spectacle of yourself,* shouting at a club.

I was ashamed.

The dancer climbed this net that hung over the audience, the strain of her every muscle clenched against the wobble of the ropes.

I hated when you'd invite me out, only to have a big group of drunk friends along with you.

I wanted to get you out of there, to spend time just the two of us, but you wanted me to come along with your big group of new friends and happy reunions.

I complained I couldn't find anything anymore at your

place, and my place was beginning to look exactly the same.

But there was the birdcage right there on the floor.

One time you cleaned your place up really nice for me.

The wicker rocking chair.

Your two The Thinker statues, one a little bigger than the other – smooth porcelain and flowers, birds painted on the orb-lamp.

Where Am I Going Now? – Was written in wide loops of lipstick on the stained-glass mirror.

Wasn't that funny?

When did you do that?

I always pictured you with other men so much that I must've liked it in some way.

The more I'd sweat you about it, even when I thought I was being casual, charming, the more funny you thought it was to make yourself ugly with makeup.

You'd layer it on thicker and thicker until you could hardly feel your face, make yourself creepy with makeup, just to sit around the apartment by yourself and laugh.

Tear-bloated, guzzling, it was difficult not to swing a smaller bottle, beer, light in your hand and coughing.

Newspapers spread out in a stiff, soft, folded mess all over the floor like the bottom of a birdcage.

Your empty birdcage balanced on top of them.

– *I did something stupid.*

Feathered masks and busts – *hello.*

Hey crooked paintings – *I did something stupid.*

I used to try to keep them straight, the crooked paintings, and they'd tilt right back into position.

Out of their sleeves, records strewn across the floor.

*

Your breath fogged the bathroom mirror.

You stood at the sink, leaning forward to press your cheek up against your cold reflection.

Your purple robe bunched at your feet, you wore only your oversized stained t-shirt.

You ran your finger through the fog of your breath on the

mirror and slowly spelled out your name.

The drain open, the tub filled slowly.

The rumble of the faucet was loud like a big engine.

Your name on the mirror slowly faded as the mirror steamed over.

You turned to the tub and – slippery, careful – you thought to move to its side.

A cloud, breath, blew out into the mirror in a sudden puff.

*

Sources

Blowup. Dir. Michaelangelo Antonioni. 1966.
Two-Lane Blacktop. Dir. Monte Hellman. 1971.
Cockfighter. Dir. Monte Hellman. 1974.
Annie Hall. Dir. Woody Allen. 1977.
Bad Timing. Dir. Nicholas Roeg. 1980.
Stillwater by Art Garfunkel, 1989.
The Bell Jar by Sylvia Plath, 1963.

*

Acknowledgments

I feel boundless gratitude to Zach Dodson whose years of encouragement and wise guidance have made this undertaking possible; Mairead Case for the close reading, patience, and thoughtful feedback; Matthew Clark for always having my back; Bobby, Theo, Melina, Mike, Sam, Victor, and Neil for gracefully accepting my disappearances; Brian Chankin and Odd Obsession for the extended rentals; Ray Pride for years of hearing me out as I untangled this; Mom for access to the hideout; Dee, Jimmy and Kurt for the material support; Jacob Knabb and Victor Giron at Curbside Splendor for their effort, trust and investment in this; Jason Mojica, Robert A.A. Lowe, and Jonathan van Herik for the world of Big Brother in which this puzzle first bloomed; and Jessica Bardsley for everything.

About the Author

Tim Kinsella (b. 1974) Chicago / Libra / Joan of Arc band